Robert B Scott

THE GOLDEN KEY

It was a dream, surely, but not such as had visited him of late.

THE GOLDEN KEY

STORIES OF DELIVERANCE

BY

HENRY VAN DYKE

The soul awakes and wondering sees
In her mild hand the golden keys.

WILLIAM BLAKE.

NEW YORK

CHARLES SCRIBNER'S SONS

1926

TO THE IMAGINED READER
GENTLE OR SIMPLE

Here are twelve tales that I have known for some time but never could find leisure to write. Now release from all sorts of official duty has set me free to work at whatever I like.

As they are brought together it appears that these are all stories of deliverance from some kind of peril or perplexity or bondage.

The book could have had as a motto: *There is always a way out.*

But this might be too sweeping,—misleading to light readers who look for a "happy ending" in tune with their own desires.

Life is not made that way. The doors of deliverance are often different from what we expected. Sometimes one that looks dark leads into liberty. However that may be, I believe that in all God's world there is no hopeless imprisonment nor endless torment.

So instead of a motto I have chosen for this book a symbol: *The Golden Key.* Take it and use it as you will.

Do not look for pointed morals here. These are only tales founded in fact, with changed names of places and people, lest the writer should offend by making public use of private affairs.

The last story is a pure romance woven on a background of reality. Separate the threads for yourself if you choose.

The first of the tales was printed in *Scribner's Magazine* in 1921. (Grateful acknowledgments to the Editor.) All the rest have been written within this year and with much joy in the writing.

HENRY VAN DYKE.

SYLVANORA
Seal Harbor
September, 1926

CONTENTS

ILLUSTRATIONS

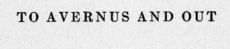

TO AVERNUS AND OUT

TO AVERNUS AND OUT

I

THE gaunt old elms of Stuyvesant Square thrust
their long, bare, ungainly arms up into the brumous
night. They seemed trying to push back the folds
of fog that hung over the city. The low houses in
their faded gentility slept blindly around the open
space, as if exhausted by the day's effort to keep up
appearances in a September hot spell. The heavy
moisture in the air gathered on the pavement like
a dim unlustrous dew. St. George's loomed dark
brown on one corner, and the Friends' Meeting-
House glimmered gray on the other. It was the
dead hour, between midnight's revelry and morning's work, when New York comes nearest to slumber.

A motor-car, shabby but smooth-running, slipped
quietly along the street that divides the park, and
stopped a few blocks farther north, at the corner of
Second Avenue opposite the grand building of the
New Hospital, where a few lights were still glowing

softly in the windows. Four men stepped noiselessly from the car and turned up the side street toward the Old Hospital with its long, low front of brick, painted dull yellow, facing a huge junk-yard, heaped full of old iron and worn-out tires and broken engines and automobiles in all stages of decay and dissolution. In the darkness it seemed like a bit of chaos, audibly haunted by lean, fierce cats.

It was not a savory region. To the west lay the placid oasis of Gramercy Park. To the east, just beyond the New Hospital, was a row of little red-brick houses with elaborate cast-iron porticoes and balconies, speaking of a time when the neighborhood had a modest residential tone. Opposite was the great High School, in gray-stone Gothic, and a little yellow Slovak church, of no namable architecture. Farther east the street ran into the populous desert of the Gas House district and the alphabetical Avenues.

But the block where the four men were walking, —going quietly but not creeping or sneaking,—was different, and had a character of its own. It was made up mostly of old stables, buildings of one or two stories: no doubt they once belonged to the mansions of Gramercy Park, and held stately barouches, luxurious victorias, and high-stepping horses. But evil times had come upon them: they were transformed into rag and bottle shops, dingy and ill-smelling garages, storehouses for all sorts of damaged goods. A few old-fashioned tenements were sandwiched in among them. In this depressed and depressing region the Old Hospital had stood for a quarter of a century, under charge of the Sisterhood of the Holy Heart, performing its patient work of ministry to the sick and wounded.

The four men advanced toward it through the misty night as persons who knew exactly where they were going and what they had to do. At least this was true of three of them,—hard-faced young gangsters of the slick New York type,—"Terry the Wop," "Red Butch," and "Slider Jim." The fourth man was older,—anywhere between forty and sixty, grizzled and very much the worse for wear. He seemed to go reluctantly, or uncertainly, as if bewildered or unwilling. He was apparently inclined to argue with his companions, but Red Butch held him by the elbow and marched him along. They did not whisper, but spoke in low voices less audible than a whisper. When they came in front of the hospital Slider Jim hurried west to the avenue to act as lookout, while the driver of the car kept watch on the eastern corner of the block. The three others slipped over the low iron railing into the shallow area and lifted the old-fashioned wooden lid which covered one of the gratings opening into the cellar.

"The stuff's in this wing,—cubby little orfice,—tin safe,—dead easy," muttered Terry.

"How d'yer know?" growled Butch.

"Sawr it," answered Terry, "w'en I was in for a mealy sicker las' week. Two big wads o' bills, bundle o' paipers, looked like lib'ty bons, an' some silver choich things,—it's a cinch!"

The older man, who had been working with some kind of a concealed flame, melting the solder which held the hinge of the grating in place, straightened up and turned around when he heard the last words.

"Nothing doing," he said. "Here's where I get off. It's too much like robbing a church. Those sisters,—good women——"

"Wot d'yer mean?" said Terry. "Hurry up with that grating, ye poor fish."

"We can lift 'er now,—go easy!" said Butch. The grating yielded to the four straining hands and was turned over quietly on the wooden cover. The

6

older man stood over the black hole, his hands twitching, his face drawn and haggard, his sunken eyes lit with dull fire.

"It's sacrilege," he muttered. "I'll be damned if I do it. And they shan't do it either. I'll——"

He lifted his head and opened his mouth as if to call out. But he was too late. A rough hand was clapped over his lips, and another clutched his throat.

"The ole stiff's goin' to pig on us," hissed Terry. "Give 'im the woiks, quick, Butch."

A piece of lead pipe wrapped in carpet makes no noise when it strikes, but it does the work. Two blows were enough. The older man went limp, sank on the edge of the black hole, and toppled over into the cellar, as a soggy stick disappears in dark water.

"Les' beat it," mumbled Terry, with his hands on the railing. But the steady Butch, listening intently, held up his finger.

"Jest a minnit," he said. "Nobody comin',—no rush,—les' put things straight."

Deftly and silently they replaced the iron grating and the wooden cover, climbed the fence, and hastened down the street with that swift unnoticeable gait, neither a run nor a walk but a kind of serpentine glide, with which a drifter "moll" disappears through a crowd when she is wanted.

At the corner the driver of the car was waiting, and Slider Jim quickly joined them.

"W'ere's the stuff?" asked the two spotters. "W'at d'yer do wid ole Woimy Reck?"

"Shut up," grunted Butch, "got nothin',—bumped the dam' squealer off,—gave him his! Now beat it."

The shabby car slid silently away eastward in the fog. Deep gloom settled on its occupants. Their late comrade lay broken on the cellar floor of the Old Hospital,—his right leg twisted under him,—a thin trickle of blood running down his chin,—dirty, haggard, dishevelled, an abject creature at the very bottom of Avernus.

II

Vernon Recklin's life had begun on high ground. The path by which he made his descent to Avernus had been a long one and a crooked one, but it had never been really an easy one. At every turn there were barriers to break through or creep around. Inherited restraints of taste and behavior; the conventions of his class and breeding; a certain sensitiveness, you might even call it fineness, in his natural liking for clean and beautiful things; and perhaps some moral quality, some instinctive admiration and respect for real goodness; all these made it difficult, at times, for him to continue the descent. He often hesitated, stopped, even turned back a few steps. But in the end he went on again. The restraints were too weak to withstand the force that pulled him,—a secret conviction that the world owed him pleasure,—entire, full, overflowing,—and a resolve that he would have it, take it, capture it if necessary,—at all events nothing should stand in the way of what he conceived to be complete self-expression, the satisfaction of all his desires.

He was the son of the highly respected minister of a rich suburban church, whose early religious enthusiasm had been crusted over by a passion for popularity and a stately eloquence, both of which he retained to the last. Vernon's mother, after piously spoiling her only child for fourteen years, passed away, and the boy was sent to a costly preparatory school and then to a costlier university, where he showed brilliant scholarship, handicapped by a fondness for gilt-edged diversions. In course of time his father died, leaving a small estate of nine or ten thousand dollars, and the young man, now his own master, entered a famous law school and graduated with honors, expensive habits, and Pistol's firm persuasion: "the world's mine oyster."

At first it seemed as if he would open it without delay or difficulty. His progress was helped somewhat by his father's friends, but even more by his own ability. He was taken into junior partnership in a steady old law firm, but it was too slow for him. He wanted more money for his growing expenses. On the strength of his reputation and his convincing personality, he set up in practice for himself. But his great expectations were not immediately realized, and he began to look around him for some means, any means, of putting them through. He formed intimacies with men of shady character, noted for their cleverness in keeping just within the fences of the law while they slipped their hands through the wires to grab whatever they could reach outside. He accepted cases which were worse than doubtful and tried them with a cynical skill which took advantage of every subterfuge. He carried it off with a certain bravado, and through all he remained agreeable in conversation, attractive in person, rather a captivating figure.

Meantime, he contracted certain private habits, in his quest of self-expression and gratification, which bit inward, and fastened a hold on him. Gambling, which was at first only a diversion, became an inveterate passion. He followed it merrily over the little green tables, and gloomily over the stock-market ticker. He liked wine and women, and in both he was regarded as a connoisseur. It was not often that he drank to excess, but his amours were notorious. They were favorite topics of conversation in the corners of the Cornucopian Club.

His father's old friends, respectable and steady persons, began to shake their heads and look grave when they spoke of the young man.

"What's wrong with Vernon Recklin?" asked Judge Plowland one day when he was lunching with Chauncey Larue at the Lawyers' Club.

"I don't know," said Larue, "but when a man's deliquescing inside, some of it usually leaks out."

And yet all the time Recklin's descending path was difficult. Not even the primroses of dalliance could make it easy. His instincts, his memories, his finer tastes, the remnants of those early beliefs which had never quite deepened into principles, revolted against some of the conditions in which he was grad-

11

ually immersed. They were not outwardly vile, but there was a close and sickening odor about them that spoke of decay.

Many a morning he woke disgusted with himself. As he came out of the cold water of his bath, he made the usual vows. "Never again. No more wine, no more women, no more gambling, no more crookedness. I'll cut it out." But the sharpness of the knife was what he could not, or would not, bear. By the next day his resolution had withered. He was as bad as ever,— perhaps a little worse. When the leaf of a good purpose falls away it leaves a scar, a hard spot.

There was one point in his career where it seemed as if a return to better ways might have been possible. Strangely enough, it was an episode in which the Scribes and Pharisees would have suspected only evil. Recklin's attachment to Madame Colette Lamy began when he was about thirty years old. She was a beautiful Frenchwoman, well born and well bred, who had fled from a drunken brutal husband in France and come to New York with her little daughter Marguerite, a brown-eyed, auburn-haired child of nearly six years. Madame Lamy had managed to save and bring with her about half her *dot* of a hundred thousand francs, and with this she set up a modest but extremely *chic* embroidery shop in one of the side streets near Madison Avenue. Almost at once it became quietly fashionable and mildly profitable. She loved gaiety and music, and went to theatres, little dances, and studio concerts, where nobody cared that she kept a shop, but everybody felt that she was charming, delicious. It was at one of these concerts that Recklin met her, and immediately became convinced that she was necessary to his happiness.

At that time he had not lost his good looks, nor the convincing magic of his manner. He was slender, erect, quick, and firm in his movements. His light-brown hair rolled above a square forehead, and his mustache of a darker brown was smooth and well cared for. His gray-blue eyes, though a little sunken, were large, very clear, and eager. His slightly pale face was without tell-tale wrinkles. He talked like an affable archangel and made love like a young Sir Launcelot.

On the moment, Madame Lamy was taken with him, and her instant liking grew into something deeper, stronger, irresistible. He appealed to her in a hundred ways, by his satire and by his sentiment, by the candor with which he owned his faults and by the scorn which he had for them, by the lightness of his touch and the urgency of his will. But she was a devout Catholic, and would not consent to marry him because the thought of divorce was horrible to her.

"*Mais non*," she murmured with her arms around his neck, "dee-ar Vairnon, I lofe you,—zat ess a sinfool zing, but it may be pardon. But *divorce,—marriage après? Non*, zat ees imposseeble, zat ees not to forgeef. Let it be as now, *cher ami*."

So it was. I am not writing a commentary on the story; I am merely telling it as it happened. Colette kept her promise,—of a loving friendship,— miraculous, incredible, but true! During the two years of their intimacy Recklin was nearer a return to the upward path than he had ever been since he started for Avernus. He liked her inexhaustible gaiety better then the grim excitement of gambling. She cheered him like good wine, and he became able to shake off the hold which stronger liquors were getting on him. Not for the world would he have had the little Marguerite see him brutalized by drink. She was so pure, so gentle, so full of a serious joy,—like a ray of light falling through the stained glass of an old cathedral window. She had one of those naturally religious souls to which the beauty of truth is revealed at birth, even as the truth of beauty is to others. In her thin, sweet, childish voice she sang through the house. Often her songs were echoes of the canticles that she had heard in church, but always with little grace-notes and quavers added to them in a quickened tempo. When these three had a day together in the country, under the lace-leafy woods of early spring, or beside the slow-breathing ocean of summer, Marguerite ran joyfully with bare feet along the edge of the foam-scallops, or danced among the wild-flowers with innocent, quaint motions like one of Fra Angelico's youngest angels.

It was an idyl; and it lasted two years. Then,—Colette caught pneumonia and died in five days. Marguerite was left by her will to the care of the Sisters of the Holy Heart. Recklin was thrown out again, alone on the slippery hillside, between the rising and the sinking path.

What would have happened if this had not come to pass? Suppose Colette had recovered and lived; suppose the wretched husband in France had drunk himself to death; suppose she had married Recklin; what would have happened?

I do not know. It is not my business. It is God's

business. He knows everything as it is. If it is certain, He knows it as certain. If it is uncertain, He knows it as uncertain. As far as possible He lets us choose, not what life will do to us, but what we will do with life. I can only tell you what Recklin did, not why he did it.

· He was very ill for three months. When he recovered,—if you call it recovery,—he had the cocaine habit. From this point Avernus-road was straighter and steeper. It seemed almost like a plunge. Of course the barriers and restraints were there, but with this magic powder he could make them disappear, forget them, escape from them. If he was going down, at least he could go comfortably and happily. So he dreamed with the help of his powder. It even gave him the illusion that he could turn back whenever he liked.

But that clean-looking white salt has a devilish power. It is full of false promises and fatal purpose. It exalts the imagination while it cripples the will. It plays havoc with the inner life long before its deadly effects on the body are visible.

Recklin looked well, even vigorous. He went about his old ways as boldly, he talked as brilliantly, he acted as carelessly as ever. But inwardly he was all gone. There was nothing to hold him back; nothing to consider, except that old desire, now stronger than ever,—the dream of self-realization, satisfaction, the draining of the full cup,—yes, of all the cups. If he had any misgivings, there was the white powder to drive them away and make everything seem easy.

His friends,—for he had some who really cared for him in spite of his debonair aloofness and the self-absorption which he concealed under his charming manner,—saw and felt what was happening to him, and a few of them tried to turn him the other way.

Mrs. Dallas Wilton, a lady whose real goodness was unfortunately handicapped by her fervent too-goodness, had what she called a "serious talk" with him.

"Dear Vernon," she said in her smoothest voice, "you *know* how *much* I loved your father, a *saintly* man! For *his* sake,—well, you know my *deep* affection for *you*. That gives me the *right* to say almost *anything* to you, doesn't it? You know there are some *very ugly* rumors going about you. Heavy drinking, high gambling, disreputable company,—I don't need to *specify*, do I? Of course I have *contradicted* the rumors as firmly as I *could* with my *limited* knowledge. But they have troubled me *awfully*. What would your *sainted father* think of them? Can't you follow in *his* footsteps? Why should you *trifle* with *temptation?*"

Recklin got up to poke the wood-fire. Then he turned smiling slightly and sat down beside her.

"Dear lady," he said with that confidential air which made him seem so far away, "how can I thank you enough for your warm defense of me? It helps a man when good women believe in him. Let me assure you that I have not been trifling with temptation, nor do I mean to do so. But as for being like my father, that I fear is far beyond me. You see, times change, and men and manners with them. Take for example the old Roman dinner customs as compared with ours."

From this he gently turned the conversation into a fascinating description of the banquets of Lucullus and Petronius Arbiter, with such details in regard to the light costumes and behavior of the flutists and harp-players as he thought Mrs. Wilton's chaste ears would relish.

"She lapped it up," he said to some of his cronies late that night, "as a cat would eat cream. Said it was *wonderful*,—so *artistic*,—wanted to *know* why *we* couldn't have something like *that* in New York! Well, we do," he added, chuckling, "but not at that old cat's house, eh, Molly?"

Tom Richards tried his hand at persuading Recklin to reform, but in a different way.

"Look here, old man," he said one night when they were walking home together from a gay college dinner, "you seem to be riding for a fall. Why don't you pull up?"

"Too much trouble." answered Recklin. "Besides, if I did I should go over the horse's head."

"It will be easier now than later," said Richards. "You're losing your best friends rather fast, and taking up with a spotty lot,—that Unterstein crowd,— rotters all of them. I beg your pardon. It's none of my business, of course,—but you know we were classmates,—I can't help speaking frankly even if you cut me for it. Have you by any chance,—you know you are very much altered since your illness,—well, I will put it straight,—have you formed one of those devilish drug-habits?"

The two men had stopped under a lamp-post on the corner of 45th Street. There was a dark flush of anger on Recklin's checks. He drew himself up and spoke with a hard, quick voice.

"Mr. Richards, I will thank you to mind your own——"

Then he paused; his face and his voice changed; he went on more slowly:

"No, Tom, I'm a fool to take it that way. What I mean is that I do thank you now for being frank with me. You have a right to do it. But you see, you don't really understand the case at all. Suppose you had lost the only thing you had ever really cared for in the world. And then suppose you found something that helped you to get on after a fashion without the lost thing, to forget yourself, to have some hours of pleasure, to carry on your work with more snap, to keep up the adventure of life and hope for better days. Wouldn't you take it? That's my case."

"It looks to me like a bad one," said Richards. "You are fooling yourself,—or that stuff is fooling you. I wish you would give it up."

"I will," answered Recklin, "but not yet,—not till I have no more need of it,—not till I find what I'm looking for, the joy of life, full up, all-round happiness, that's what I'm after,—eh, old man? Then I'll cut out all exciting things and join you on the steady path,—I promise you! Well, here I'm going west,—I have a date at Regenwetter's with a couple of friends. So long, Tom, and thank you again."

He turned into 45th Street, walking rather heavily with dragging steps, as if he were trudging through sand. When he got beyond Seventh Avenue and the glittering zone of lights, he paused in the shadowy middle of the block, took a little phial from his vest pocket, shook a pinch of white powder into his left hand, and snuffed it up eagerly.

"That makes me feel better," he said to himself. "Poor old Tom, what does he know? But some day I'll keep my promise, and surprise him."

The surprise came; but not as Recklin had dreamed it. Three sudden plunges carried him completely out of the world in which he still lived, though on sufferance. First there was the celebrated Unterstein divorce case,—collusion, bigamy, false papers,—in which he was so far implicated that he was advised to withdraw from the Bar Association as having disregarded the ethics of the legal profession. Then there was the famous poker game at Stingfield's place, in which young Harmon Garrett lost fifty thousand dollars in a night. Recklin was in the party, and held one of the I. O. U.'s. He said he never intended to cash it. Nothing was proved against him; but the

game was undoubtedly queer; marked cards were
found. Recklin may have known nothing about
them, but he was a winner in the game,—and was
asked to resign from the Cornucopian Club. Finally
came the notorious scandal at Alty Devens' week-end
party. Of course, Cissy Devens was a fool girl, and
loved playing with fire. But that was no excuse.
There are some things that a man simply must not
do,—at least with people of a certain standing. So
Recklin was cast out, finally and with scorn, from the
golden sunshine of society into the region of alternat-
ing glare and obscurity, where the high white lights
flash and flare, and the low red lights wink in the
darkness.

The upper world to which he had been attached
knew him no more, passed him in the street without
recognition. The underworld took note of him and
waited for him. The Untersteins and the Stingfields
welcomed him and sympathized with him against
"the Pharisees." When he was sober their talk made
him rather sick. But when he was slightly intoxicated
it pleased him.

"After all," he told himself, "hypocrisy is the only
thing in the world that is absolutely wrong."

From the club he dropped to the café and the cabaret, and from them to the unmitigated saloon and the "broad" hotel. His talents and accomplishments did not seem to be extinguished, but only perverted. He put them at the service of any one who would pay for them, and at first he made enough money to keep him in comfort and a kind of luxury. He was "legal adviser" to a firm which dealt in fraudulent divorces. He conducted the "propaganda" for certain predatory stock corporations. He was hand in glove with many members of the swell mob. But his profits did not last long: he spent lavishly and gambled wildly. The solemn Wall Street tapeworm ate up most of his gains.

The swell mob, the higher circle of graft, is not given to permanent personal affections. It is divided into two classes: those who contrive big hauls and get away with them into some new country; and those who have the misfortune to be "pinched" and go to jail. Recklin was not in either class. He never got away with big money. He never was caught and convicted. Consequently he fell between the stools, and was always an alien in this section of Alsatia,—regarded with contempt by those who had their ambitions set on climbing toward Belgravia, and with mistrust by those who were confirmed picaroons. He was constantly displeased and angered both by the contempt and by the mistrust. Avernus-road was far from pleasant in those years. But he was too proud, or too weak, to turn back.

It was easier, in fact it was inevitable to go on downward, into membership of one of the criminal "gangs" which included clever thieves and bold highwaymen, grafters, and gunmen of all kinds. Here his natural abilities, his legal knowledge, and a certain deftness of hand which he curiously developed, gave him a kind of reputation. But it was not leadership; he was not of the tribe; the story of his respectable past,(much exaggerated,) clung to him and made him a suspect. He was not bad enough. He had curious prejudices,—against blasphemy of the name of Jesus, and dirtiness, and violence to women, and assassination,—which marked him as an outsider at heart. He kept on with the gang, because it seemed impossible to do anything else. But the grimy conditions of his life revolted him; often he was almost crazy to break away from it.

Then the Great War came and seemed to offer him a chance at least to die with honor. By a miraculous effort he braced up physically, cut out drugs and drink, made himself clean, and enlisted under an assumed name, giving his age as twelve years younger than it was. He served with credit in France, won a decoration for heroic conduct in the field, was mustered out, and came home to—what?

A parade,—and then oblivion!

He had been severely gassed and his lungs and heart were permanently weakened. His nerve was broken. He was incapable of continuous hard labor. Even if he could have done it, there was none for him to do. No man cared for his soul. He struggled for a while, and then sagged back, naturally and sullenly, into his old habits and the old gang. But now he came at their price, on a lower level. They used him for what he was worth. He was only forty-five, but he looked sixty-five. It was for this reason that they twisted his name into "Wormy Reck." He was really a learned slave, an unvenerable Helot to those nimble and ruthless young brigands. They did not trust him, but they made his brains and his skill serve them. He hated it, but he could see no way out of it.

So the taskmaster's whip drove him down, deeper and deeper, until at last he lay like a discarded thing in the pit of Avernus, abandoned to death in the cellar of the Old Hospital.

III

Sister Colette Marguerite was the youngest nurse in the hospital, full of energy and zeal. It was part of her duty in that month of September to make the early morning round, unlocking the front doors and putting up the window-shades. It was still quite dark in the lower hallway, so she carried a light in her steady hand. As she passed the cellar-stair it seemed as if she heard a slight sound below like some one groaning or breathing raucously. It startled her, but she was not afraid. She went down the steps quietly and opened the creaking door.

Perhaps it was the noise, perhaps it was the light falling on his face, that penetrated Vernon Recklin's stupor and brought him half-awake. Painfully he propped himself on his right arm and stared silent at the vision in the doorway. It was a dream, surely, but not such as had visited him of late. Was it an angel with pure face and compassionate eyes, sent to warn him? No, the dark robe, the black veil folded over the white cap, the linen band across the brow, —it was one of the sisters,—he was caught at last! He moaned with pain and sank back into his stupor.

The little sister ran swiftly for help. They carried

the inert body up-stairs, and laid it, half-undressed, on a bed. The doctor came quickly and made an examination. Evidently the right leg had a compound and comminuted fracture, and the left collar-bone was broken. There was also a bruise behind the ear made by a heavy blunt instrument,—certainly a brain-concussion, perhaps a slight fracture of the skull,—impossible to tell yet.

"The injuries are serious," said the doctor, "but not hopeless, unless he is one of those drug-fiends with a ruined constitution. That's what he looks like,—yes, see, here's a bottle of the stuff in his pocket. Sister, this time I reckon you have caught a real burglar, a 'bad 'un.'"

She shook her head and answered gently: "Have we any right to judge him before we have heard him? He looks to me more like a victim. Perhaps some one tried to rob and murder him, and then threw him down the cellar to get him out of the way and put suspicion on him. Anyhow, no matter what he is, we must do our best to heal his wounds. That is what the hospital is for, isn't it?"

The difference of opinion in regard to the man continued. The police were called, but could throw no clear light on the affair. They agreed that he must be kept where he was, under surveillance, while they "investigated." So the doctor took charge of the case, and Sister Colette Marguerite of the man. From the first she seemed to consider him her own *trouvaille*, her special property, her ward temporal and spiritual.

There was something that drew her toward him in spite of his degradation,—a filmy thread of undefined reminiscence,—something that she felt she had lost and could not quite recall. She knew by instinct that his life was stained and dishonored, yet she was sure that in some strange way it was connected with her, belonged to her. There was nothing in his threadbare face that she could recognize; but now and then a tone in his voice seemed familiar, a look in his faded eyes awakened vague memories that puzzled her.

"It is only a foolish imagination, I guess," she acknowledged to the Mother Superior. "Probably I never saw the man before. Certainly I never knew any one named Victor Roberts, as he calls himself. But, Mother, may it not be that God sent him to me to save, to be my first convert? Will you permit me to make that my special intention and do all that I can to fulfil it?"

The Mother Superior smiled a little at the phrase

"God sent him"; it was assuredly an extraordinary method of Divine sending, to dump a man in the cellar like a sack of coal; but it was possible,—all things are possible. The sincerity and devotion of the little sister were beyond doubt; she had the vocation,—and she was a clever nurse too. So she had her way, and looked after the wounded man as if he were her child.

The doctor, of course, directed the case from the surgical and medical side; and it was a long one and a difficult one, but it finally began to improve. The other sisters took their share of the nursing, of course, when their turns came; and they did their duty faithfully, though none of them especially liked the man. But it was the little Sister Marguerite who adopted him and cared for his soul and undertook to win it back from Avernus.

After the first week he had a relapse, and was unconscious or delirious for many days. When reason returned to him he was very silent and passive; he did not seem to care what became of him. His injuries pained him atrociously, but the clean sheets and the cool bathing, the order and quiet of the room, gave him a comfort that he had not known for years. Most of all the friendly presence, the firm, cool touch

29

of the little sister's hands, soothed and refreshed him.
Even when he was feverish and fractious, hungering
for his familiar devil-drug, she could make him quiet.
He talked little, but his eyes followed her with the
questioning, trusting look which you sometimes see
in the eyes of a good dog, beginning to grow a soul.

"Surely I know her," he thought vaguely, "some-
where in the world we have been together before this.
Where have I seen those wide brown eyes, that curly
russet hair which sometimes shows under her coif?
And her voice, so light and clear? Ah, I have it now.
I will ask her what her real name is."

She answered the question very simply. "You
know in this Congregation of the Holy Heart we are
allowed to keep our baptismal names. Mine is Colette Marguerite, — after my mother and Sainte
Marguerite,—it is the name of a flower, too."

"Yes," he sighed contentedly, settling back on his
pillow, "I know,—I mean, it is a very pretty name.
I like it. Thank you, Sister Marguerite."

As he grew better, their conversations were longer.
She talked to him of what was happening in the hospital and outside, and of her education at the con-
vent-school in the Bronx, and of what she could remember of her childhood and her mother.

"Best of all were the days that we spent in the country, in the spring or the summer. There was a friend, a splendid man, who used to go with us and play wonderful games with me in the woods and build sand-forts on the seashore. I can't recollect his name but I shall never forget him. I wish I could see him again."

The man listened as if entranced by tales of wonderful adventure. He encouraged her to go on, but he told her nothing of himself. He was afraid and ashamed. He felt like a bad child whom his mother comforteth.

Thus skilfully and slowly the little sister laid her lines and intrenchments round him for her great intention, the capture of his soul, her first conversion. She won his confidence. She had an ally within the fortress. Then, one Sunday afternoon, she advanced to the direct attack.

"My friend, I tell you all about me. You listen, but you tell me nothing about you. Why is that?"

"You know my name already. You see what I am. There is nothing more worth telling."

"But it is yourself that I want to know about. Your name is nothing,—it can be put on or off as you please. Tell me about yourself. Have you been a bad man?"

"Bad?" he said in a low, shaking voice. "That is not the word for it. Say wicked, worthless, miserable. I will tell you, since you ask it, what I have done."

"No," she interrupted gently, laying her hand on his arm, "that is not what I ask. Those sins are not for me to hear. They are for the priest in the confessional,—they are for God to forgive. Will you tell them to Him?"

"Is there a God to forgive such a man as me?" The tears ran down the little sister's face.

"There is, there is," she urged, "I know it. I am as sure of it as that we are here. Hasn't he spared your life? Hasn't he sent you here to me?"

"Yes,—perhaps it may be so,—but for what?"

"To save you," she pleaded. "He sent you to me for that. Listen; let me tell you."

Then she unfolded the mysteries of her simple faith; the wideness of the heavenly mercy, like the wideness of the sea; the seeking love of the Holy Heart of Jesus, who died on the cross between two thieves and took one of them with him to Paradise. Recklin had heard it all a hundred times before, but never on this wise, never with such intense reality as if it had happened in this very city, never so close to the dark background of his own downward path.

He yielded. He turned. He faced the light. His heart opened.

"Yes," he said quietly, "I'll do what you say,—make confession, repent, believe,—the priest may come to-morrow. Only you must not go far away from me, Sister Marguerite, for what I believe most of all is that God sent me to *you* to be saved."

Father Read was a wise and kind old man of much experience, who knew how to build on a frail foundation without crushing it by too heavy pressure. His instructions from day to day were brief but adequate, —the meaning of faith, and penitence, and the sacraments. Yes, confession was needful, of course; but it was always sacred and would never be violated; and it was not necessary to confess other people's offenses, only your own. There was no fear of betraying others. Baptism need not be repeated. The way into membership of the church would be open after a few weeks of teaching and trial. Divine assistance would be given in answer to prayer. Thus the upward path was made clear; and the fallen man, beginning to climb with the remnant of his strength, felt that the day of his deliverance had come and held fast to his deliverer, the little Sister Marguerite.

She was filled with humble joy. Her heart sang canticles of gratitude for her first convert, the wreck that had been sent to her to be saved, the lost sheep that she had brought back to the Shepherd. But there were times when she had her fears and misgivings.

"Have I been too proud?" she asked Father Read one day after her own innocent confession. "Have I trusted too much in my own intention and effort? Do you think he is really converted and saved? Do you think he will stand fast? Will he be able to resist temptation after he goes back into the world?"

"My child," said the old man, knowing more of life in general and of Vernon Recklin's kind of life in particular than she would ever know, "daughter, you must cast away pride and put your confidence in God. He is almighty; the devil is only strong. You must rely on the grace of the sacrament, on the mercy of Providence, to guide your convert through the temptations that will surely meet him. If they are too strong for him,—and it may be so,—Providence will surely find a way of deliverance for him. But meantime see that you give him all the help you can."

So she did. Every day she talked with him cheerfully and confidently, made little plans for the future, fixed the times when he should come back to see her and bring her his report. It was almost like a mother preparing her boy to go away to school. Through her friends outside she had secured a lodging for him and a good place to work.

On the morning when he was to leave the hospital she took him to the altar of the Virgin Mary where she had lit the seven candles.

"See how bright they burn," she said; "that is because it is so still here. But out in the wind you would need to shield them. Now, my friend, I am going to give you three things that will keep the light in your soul from being blown out. Every day you must say the 'Hail Mary.' "

"I say it with all my heart,—*ave Maria plena gratia.*"

"Then you must say the *Pater noster* every evening."

"I do say it, and I'll never forget,—*our* Father."

"Then there is a special prayer that I want you to say every morning. Please repeat it now after me."

They bent their heads before the altar and folded

35

their hands, he with knotted fingers, she with smooth palms. The two voices alternated, one light and clear, the other husky and tremulous.

> "Vouchsafe, O Lord—"
> *vouchsafe, O Lord,*
> "To keep me this day—"
> *to keep me this day,*
> "Without sin—"
> *without sin.*
> "O Lord in thee have I trusted,"
> *O Lord in thee have I trusted,*
> "Let me never be confounded"—
> *let me never be confounded.*

"Now you must go, my friend," said the little sister. "He sent you to me, and he will keep you safe." But she wept and trembled behind the green door of the hospital as Vernon Recklin went down the steps.

As he turned the corner of the avenue, Terry and two others of the old gang met him. By the "wireless" of the underworld they knew what had happened in the hospital, and were waiting for him.

"Hello," they cried, "here y'are, all cleaned up. Well, Butch is pinched, and Slider's pinched, and we want you, old squealer. So come along wid us."

"No," he said, facing the two who spoke, while

The two voices alternated, one light and clear, the other husky and tremulous.

Terry slipped behind him, "I haven't squealed on you, and don't mean to. But I won't go with you,— never."

Two pistol-shots cracked from the gun in Terry's pocket.

"You've got yours now," he cried as he disappeared with his companions in the noon-day flood of people.

Vernon Recklin sank to the pavement, two bullets close to his heart. A little crowd quickly gathered round him. Some one lifted his head.

"Tell her," he labored as the blood rose in his throat, "Sister Colette Marguerite,—Old Hospital, —tell her—I'm *out—saved!*"

His hand made the sign of the cross, and dropped on his breast.

A CAST-OFF SON

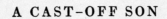

A CAST-OFF SON

WHETHER the following tale be true altogether, or only in part, I know not. Of a part we may be sure, because it is written in a scripture of high authority. The rest is open to doubt. I recount it as told me by a ragged Arabian story-teller in Damascus,—a city wherein are many romancers, and some liars.

So without further preface, to our story.

It begins with a man called Abram Ben Terah, a dweller in Ur of the Chaldees many ages ago. His name signifies "exalted father"; and this indeed was his character, for at bottom he was passionately patriarchal. He craved nothing else so much as to be the father of a family and to hand down his seed to many generations.

At the same time he was of a roving, venturous temper, not indeed brave, nor except on one occasion warlike, but fondly addicted to travels and explorations in strange lands. These brought him

41

into many a strait and perilous pass, out of which he escaped, not always with credit, but always with a sound skin, and often with great increase of goods and flocks and herds, for he was a master hand with sheep and cattle. In his rovings he was not a servant of idols nor a consulter of necromancers, but he was obedient unto his unseen God, whom he called JAH, and who had promised to make of him a great nation, possessor of many of the lands through which he journeyed. On the fulfilment of this promise Abram was firmly bent, and willing to apply himself with vigor to its consummation.

You should know that in his father's house his eyes had fallen on his half-sister, a lively and buxom Summerian maid with bright brown eyes and fulvous hair,—a girl of such high mettle and quick spirit that she was called Sarai, the meaning of which is "contentious." She was much given to laughing, whether in sport, or in scorn. But of her temper the adventurous Abram recked little. With his eyes his desire had fallen on the fair Sarai, and he proposed to make her his wife, in order that the heavenly promise might be fulfilled.

Now among us it is not lawful or seemly that a man should marry his father's daughter. But who are we that we should find fault with the manners of the patriarchs and the custom of the country wherein they were bred?

So Terah gave his consent and his fair daughter Sarai to Abram, his adventurous son, and they took the road together, under the favor of Jah, for a long life of companionry. They dwelt in tents, or in a guest-free palace, as the case might be. Together they endured hardships and dangers. Together they sported and took their pleasure. Sarai laughed, and Abram grieved at the delay of his hopes as a patriarch. Ever as they journeyed, their flocks and herds, their men servants and maid servants increased and multiplied about them. But no son was born in the tent of Sarai.

Then she was vexed by the evident discontent of her husband. His chagrin irked her. Now she had among her servants a young maid brought from Egypt whose name was Hagar, which means "flight." She was slim and fine and strong, like the women of Egypt,—very pleasant to look upon. Her skin was of the color of old ivory, and her eyes were long and still like pools of night with stars in them.

Sarai brought this maid to Abram and said in short:

"She is mine. I give her to you. Take her, and do as you like with her."

So Abram did.

In due time Hagar had a son whom she named Ishmael, which signifies, "God Hears," because, said she:

"God has heard my affliction."

Here, at last, we come to the gist of the tale, which has to do with the fate of the son of Hagar. He grew apace, slender and supple as a young leopard. The charm of Egypt was in his look, the dream of the desert on his dark face. For all his leanness he was full of vigor, courage, and skill; a hardy rider, a fearless hunter, sure with the bow, infallible with the spear; an ardent youth and high-tempered, yet most lovable and winning in his ways. His sober-sided father wondered and doted on him, and of his mother's heart he was the light and the joy.

Matters continued in this way for some years. The lad was daily fretted by the strict rule of the family, and by Sarai's heavy hand and scornful laugh for him and his mother. But in the main he was content with what was given him; and Abram, half-content, grew so fond that he thought to make this slim, eager Ishmael the heir of all his worldly gear and of the patriarchal blessing. On this point the good man consulted his God.

"Oh that Ishmael might live before thee," prayed the patriarch.

"Nay," answered Jah, very distinctly, "this is not my intention. You must wait and do your duty. Your wife whom I now name Sarah, (that is, the Princess,) shall bear you a son. His shall be the heritage. Your name shall henceforth be Abraham, (that is, father of a multitude,) for from you shall come nations and kings of peoples. Ishmael, whom you love, cannot be one of the Patriarchs, yet he also shall have a blessing, but different."

So Abraham was obedient. And in due time, as it were by a miracle, Sarah being well stricken in years, her son was born. Then she was uplifted and proud, so that her hand upon the household was even heavier than before. She named her child Isaac, (that is, "laughter.")

At this time Ishmael was about fourteen years old, and in a foolish hour he mocked at the infant Isaac who wept loudly on the day that he was weaned. So the Princess Sarah was very angry and not minded to suffer this indignity from the son of a handmaid.

"Cast out this Egyptian woman with her off-spring," she cried to her husband, "for I cannot bear the sight of them."

This grieved Abraham to the heart, for he was tender in his affections and a man who loved peace and quietness. He looked down his nose, which was long and hooked. Two tears fell upon the un-melting snow of his beard as he pleaded humbly with the Princess, for the thing pleased him not.

"Must it be so?" said he. "Do you not remember that you——"

But she cut him short with "It must be so!"

Then Abraham knew that obedience was the duty of a patriarch. Very early in the morning he rose up with a heavy heart, and called Hagar and his first-born son. He took bread and a skin of water and put them upon the mother's shoulder and sent her forth with the boy into the wilderness.

Here we take our leave of Abraham and his Princess, to follow the fortune of Hagar and the lad named "God Hears."

It seemed as if they must be gone out of God's hearing in that day, for they were cast off, by no fault of theirs, unless it were that young, ignorant mocking of the baby patriarch by the boy Ishmael.

A CAST-OFF SON

Now the wilderness where they went was a horrid place, fearful and very wearisome. The rocks were black around them and the gullies deep and dreadful. Green grass was there none, but a few blood-red pimpernels and pallid rock-roses withered between the stones. No trees were there, but only twisted thorny billâns and apples of Sodom with smooth fruit full of bitter dust.

Through this dry despair of earth the outcasts plodded on, not knowing whither they went nor where they might find a refuge in the world. In the tormented thorn-thickets foxes barked, and from a black gully there came the fierce snickering of a hyena. Hand in hand for comforting went mother and son. The sun beat upon them with a fervent heat. They were footsore and outdone.

"Is it too hard for you, son?" asked the mother.

"No, mother," said the boy, "but I crave a drop of water."

Hagar took the flapping bottle of goatskin from her back, shook it, pressed it, wrung it. It was empty as a last year's bird's-nest. There was not even a drop of water in it. Then the lad, spent with travail and thirst, fell at her feet in a swoon.

"Where is God, that He does not hear?"

With breaking heart she strained to lift her son and laid him under the shade of a bush. His face was paler than the greenish-white poison-flowers of the datura above him. She withdrew from him about the flight of an arrow, and covered her head.

"He is dying," she wailed, and as she wept she felt the broken pieces of her heart fall down within her. "How can I bear to look upon the death of my first-born child?"

Then there was a footfall beside her, and she looked up to see a messenger of the God whose eyes had been upon the fatherless and the outcast in their wandering.

"Fear not," said the messenger, "since He who sent me has heard the voice of the lad. Take him up in your arms once more, for he shall live and shall become a great nation."

Then Hagar felt her heart made whole again within her. She lifted the slender boy, holding him close on her breast; and as she followed the messenger her eyes were cleared of weeping, so that she saw a pure fountain of water springing out among the rocks. There she laved the face and the wrists of the lad and gave him gently to drink, a drop at a time. Presently he sat up, and looked at his

mother, and spoke,—he whose voice she had thought
never to hear again.

"What place is this, mother?"

"Son, I know not," said she, "and I care not,
since it is here that you have come back to me from
the grave."

For many days after this they went on with the
messenger, who showed them the way, and found
shelter for them, and fed them with food convenient
for them, and made their path smooth,—yet not too
smooth! It was still a venture. There were chances
to take and dangers to face, rough hills to climb and
strangers to encounter who might be enemies.
Every day was a new day, full of fresh hazards and
novel scenes. In all this the boy rejoiced and was
glad. It made him a man. He rose to meet it as a
falcon rises to meet the wind of the wilderness, feeling the power of his wings.

So they travelled through the land that is called
Negeb, where there were green vales of pasture between the long stony ridges, and black clustering
tents of herdsmen, and wells of water with cattle
gathered round them, and ancient towns of gray
stone, and caravans of camels rocking on their way
to Egypt.

Then they turned eastward, rounding the Sea of Bitterness by the south, crossing many ravines and wadis, and climbing at last by a steep way to the high table-land that cast its shadow from the east over the dead salt lake. Here on a knurly cliff, safe set from all attack and looking far across the dismal valley and its lifeless sea, they saw a town of gray stone, larger, stronger, more ancient than the others,—Kir Moab, the head city of that wild country. To the gate of this city the messenger led Hagar and Ishmael, and there left them.

"Farewell," he said, "my errand is done. God be with you and hear you."

With that he was gone in a moment as if carried away by the air; and Hagar with her son stood wondering at the city gate. Within they saw an old, old man who came to meet them followed by many servants. He was tall and stately; his white beard fell below his girdle; his brown cloak was of finest camel's hair; his white head-cloth was of silk, bound with a circle of twisted gold, and about his neck was a golden chain, for he was very rich, the chief man of the city and of the tribes roundabout. They called him Melek, that is " King." He greeted the strangers courteously and eyed them sharply.

"Who are you?" he asked. "From what country do you come on foot and without protection?"

"Sire," answered Hagar meekly, in her lovely voice, "we have been under protection of a messenger of God, but he has left us at your royal gate. I am a woman of Egypt and this is my son. We come from the tents of Abram Ben Terah in the land of Canaan."

At this Melek's dark brows drew together.

"I have heard of that man," he said, "and I like him not. He is a rover who grows rich. He gathers cattle that he has not bred and feeds them in pastures where his fathers were not known. Has he sent you hither to spy out the land?"

"Not so, my lord," she answered in her lovely voice, bowing down to the ground in shame, "verily not so, but far otherwise. Abram has cast me off, with this his first-born son. He has sent us away into the wilderness into the hands of chance. We shall not look upon his face again."

"That is well," said Melek, "for he who casts off his own flesh and blood is not worthy to be looked upon. But there is no such thing as chance, woman! All is written. Doubtless the messenger of Him who writes has led you to this city where God has taught

us never to deny hospitality to the stranger. Come
in to the house of the king."

It was a fair, large house, though the furniture
of it was rude. Yet it was full of comfort to the
travellers, and after they were bathed from the
stains of their journey and clad in fresh raiment,
they were abundantly refreshed with venison and
bread of fine flour and bowls of goat's milk and cups
of wine made from the grapes of Eschol. And so to
bed when they had supped, Hagar with the women,
Ishmael with the men. Thus it continued for some
days, and daily they found more favor in the eyes
of Melek. For Hagar was yet very comely, and
Ishmael was a brave, upstanding lad, ready for anything.

On a certain day Melek sought to test him.

"What can you do?" he asked. "What manner
of life are you for?"

"My lord," said the lad boldly, "I am a hunter."

"At your age!" laughed the old man. "Can you
draw the bow? Can you thrust the spear?"

"Sire," answered the lad, "I can try."

"Good," said Melek, who had been a mighty
hunter in his youth. "You shall have your trial
whether you are fit to stand before the king. A

black-maned lion has been rending and devouring our flocks in the country beyond the river Arnon. He is yours for the hunting. Will you go alone? Or shall I send a company with you?"

"My lord," said Ishmael, "this lion is for my own bow and my own spear. But two companions I would have with me, to carry my body home if evil should befall me."

So the three rode forth at daybreak, and passed over Arnon at the setting of the sun, and slept under an oak, but saw no lion. The next day they rode up the valley, and made a wide cast around it to northward, but saw no lion. That night they slept under a terebinth, and heard a lion roaring far away. Before the sun was up the next day they rode eastward to the edge of the desert. There in a rocky hollow where a small spring flowed and made a green cup of grass, they heard and saw the lion.

He was big like a bull, and the hair of his head and neck was long and black, very terrible in aspect. His fangs and his claws were bloody; his lips and his tawny breast were dabbled with red. He was rending and tearing a ram of the flock that he had carried off. He growled as he ate, like a fierce feeder.

"Here is my lion," said Ishmael, dismounting. "Bide you here while I go and get him."

So the two companions held the horses while Ishmael crept craftily among the rocks to the rim of the green cup, where the musky smell of the lion came to his nostrils plainly, for the wind blew toward him. Then he fitted an arrow to the bow-string, drew it to the head, and let it go. But the wind in the hollow was curving, and it veered the arrow so that it struck the ground beside the lion. He lifted his black head growling, and stood up to look about him.

Then Ishmael drew another arrow, and sent it swift and strong as a levin-bolt, and it struck the lion in the flank. He sprang high in fury, caught sight of the two men with the horses, and went leaping and bounding up the hill toward them, roaring as he ran. When he was near to the rock where Ishmael sheltered, the lad stepped out to face him, holding his tough spear stiff and strong. It caught the lion full in the throat, where neck meets breast, and pierced him to the heart so that the blood gushed forth. Man and beast fell together in the hot scarlet flood.

The two companions came running down the hill

with drawn knives, thinking to find their captain dead. But it was the lion that was dead, and Ishmael was alive, though sorely buffeted and a little torn. So they took the skin of the great beast with his black head and rode back to Kir Moab rejoicing.

When Melek saw them coming he was very glad, for he had been troubled, loving the young man exceedingly, and fearing for his safety. But now the lion-skin, borne on a pole between two of the horses, made the old chief happy and sure that all was well. He came out to meet the young man and embraced him, kissing him on both cheeks.

"Now you have been tested," said the old man, "and you are worthy to stand before the king,— nay, to sit beside him, for you shall be my heir, since God has taken all my proper sons from me by death."

The people were glad when they heard this, for Ishmael had won all their liking and they saw in him a man of valor to lead them against their enemies. The heart of Hagar sang a little song of joy. The king, who had been long widowed, looked upon her comeliness and observed her amiable nature with growing inclination to make her his wife. Though she was a little mistrustful of aged men, yet for her son's sake and because she saw that Melek was of a generous and noble disposition, she was not unwilling to yield to his desire. So she did, and she warmed and comforted his old age.

Ishmael now lived as a Prince in all freedom and merriment. The dew of the morning was upon him and he rode and hunted where he would. His people loved him and followed him. The hand of the neighbor tribes was against him because he was wild and masterful; but then his hand was also against them, and it was the quicker and stronger, so that he went where he pleased and took what he needed. Melek gave the young sheik his own daughter and his sister's daughter to wife. The days of Ishmael were passed in hunting and raiding and his nights were filled with good cheer and repose.

On a certain day Hagar said to her husband, "Sire, I have a request."

"Name it," said he.

"I would fain go down to Egypt," she answered.

"For what purpose?" he asked.

"To see my former home," she replied, "and my old friends, and to fetch a wife for my son."

"But why?" asked the old sheik, surprised.

"He is already well provided with wives. Why bring another from a far country?"

"It was my own country, sire," answered Hagar with tears in her voice, "and the damsel will speak the tongue of my childhood; that will be pleasant to hear."

So Melek, being much at ease and full of kind, grateful thoughts, agreed to her petition.

"You shall go," he said, "and God be with you. Only tarry not too long, for I am old."

Hagar was mounted upon a white, smooth-pacing camel, with plentiful gear for the journey, and a retinue of servants to protect and serve her. In high state she rode down to Egypt.

There she was made welcome and spent two years in visiting and colloguing with her friends,—looking always for a fit consort for her son. Among all the maidens she found but one to her mind, the daughter of Pharaoh's chief huntsman, a fine, fearless damsel; clean-limbed, deep-bosomed, fleet-footed; with hair of a soft blackness and long eyes like pools of night with stars in them. She was a huntress by inheritance.

To the father of this damsel Hagar spoke wisely of her son's wealth and prospects, and of the dowry.

To the damsel herself she spoke of those things which women tell to one another in whispers. So the matter was concluded to the satisfaction of both parties, and Asenath rode on the white camel with Hagar back to the highlands of Moab.

In the meantime the old king had passed away, at peace, in the ripeness of his years, and Ishmael ruled in his stead. He it was who came to meet the women in the gate of Kir Moab, with the white silk keffiyeh on his head, bound with the agal of twisted gold. When Asenath saw him she was enamoured of him, and to her his soul leaped as a deer to its covert. She came into his house with rejoicing and the other wives made her welcome in the wedding-feast.

(Here my ragged story-teller eyed me a moment and interrupted his tale to say, "Be not offended at the number of the wives, Effendi, for it was the custom of the country; and your own Scriptures say that God winked at those times of ignorance.")

Thenceforward the days of Ishmael ran like a river full of water, now dashing in the swift rapids, now flowing smooth and sleepy in pleasant places. With riding and raiding, with hunting and herding, with cherishing his people and beating down his enemies, he was ever busy and had great joy of life. Twelve strong sons were born in his house, and as these grew to manhood they rode at their father's side, his bodyguard in the fight, his scouts in the chase.

Bears and lions he killed for prey; ostriches for their feathers; fallow deer and gazelles for food. The fleet wild ass of the Arabian desert could not escape him, for he learned to snare it with a rope. For sport he rode one, a noble beast of white, so that men said, "Lo, the wild ass of the desert is coming," and they fled away to hide.

Far and wide he roamed in Araby, and it is reported that he saw many wondrous things which have now vanished. He saw the Phœnix, bird of red and gold, which lives a hundred years, and builds a nest of fragrant boughs on which it is burned, and the young Phœnix springs from its ashes. He saw the Amazons, warrior-women, who suffer no man in their island kingdom; but by night they cross the water to Chaldea that they may find lovers. These women Ishmael liked not, because each of them had one breast seared away, in order to use the bow and shield better.

Of these marvels I speak not with assurance, but

only to show that the life of Ishmael was wild and venturesome. When he was beyond fifty years old, he went raiding in the land of Canaan where he was born. His twelve tall sons rode by his bridle-rein. As he came toward Hebron, by the oaks of Mamre, where Abraham was wont to camp, he saw a man of middle age and gentle aspect, sitting in the shade of a large black tent, meditating.

To this man Ishmael rode swiftly, with his twelve sons following. Then the man was afraid, for he suspected violence. But Ishmael knew him by his long hooked nose, and saluted him with courtesy.

"Fear not," he said, "we come in peace. I think you are my half-brother Isaac. I am Ishmael, the eldest son of Abraham, and these are my twelve sons."

"We thought you dead," murmured the patriarch Isaac.

"Not yet," laughed Ishmael. "And your mother Sarah,—is she still living, and is it well with her?"

"She died some years ago," sighed the patriarch, "and my father buried her in the cave of Macpelah, near by."

"God rest her soul," said Ishmael. "But is our father yet in the land of the living?"

"He married again," said the patriarch, "and by this wife Keturah he had six sons. To these he gave gifts and sent them away into the east country.

"Yesterday he died, and to-day we bury him in the cave of Macpelah. Will you break bread with me, brother, in my tent, and then go with me to lay our father to rest?"

Ishmael thought for a moment and said gravely, "With good-will and peace."

So when they had buried their father and set the great stone at the mouth of the cave, the half-brothers gave each other the parting kiss of peace, and Ishmael said to Isaac:

"Now I know that there is no anger in my heart toward our father. For though he cast me off, and sent me away into the wilderness with my mother to perish, God has turned it all to good for us and delivered us into freedom and a large joy. I could never have borne the burden of being a patriarch. Freedom is my breath."

Here my ragged story-teller broke off and waited for his reward. I asked him if that was the end of the tale.

"There are other chapters, Effendi," he replied,

"but this is enough to show that the Almighty delivers men by strange ways. Ishmael was the father of the Arabians, and we believe that he lies buried beside Hagar in the holy city of Mecca."

THE SWEET INFLUENCE OF
THE PLEIADES

THE SWEET INFLUENCE OF
THE PLEIADES

HE was not an astrologer,—one of those people who think that our life is controlled by the stars and that a man's destiny can be read in his horoscope. Herschel Wheaton had too much science and too much Yankee common sense to take any interest in such superstitions as that.

But undoubtedly he believed in his plain, practical way,—yes, we may even say he knew by experience, —that the stars have a certain real influence upon our lives through our thoughts and emotions.

"Just as the mountains defend us," he would say, "by the feeling of strength and security they give us when we look at them; just as the ocean attracts and overawes us by its breadth, its mystery, its changeful sameness; so the stars guide us by their beautiful order, their shining obedience to inflexible laws, their steady movement on far roads. It's all in the Bible, you know, this idea of our getting something real from Nature, from the works of God which are as divine as his words. The mountains stand for his righteousness; the sea for his deep, strange judgments. 'The stars in their courses fought against Sisera.' What does that mean? Not astrology,—that's nonsense! Sisera was a robber-chief, a wild, lawless man. The sight of the big, calm stars shining over him while he rode on his fierce raid humbled his pride and weakened his nerve. So his courage broke and he lost the fight. I suppose that is how the stars fought against Sisera."

You must not infer from this little sermon on Scripture that Wheaton was a preacher. He was something much more practical and difficult. He was the principal of a great seminary for girls and young women in Brooklyn, and with his wife he conducted the big boarding-house for out-of-town pupils which stood next to the massive gray mid-Victorian building of the Institute.

This double task was by no means an easy, soothing business. It was as full of trials, tribulations, and surprises as a thicket of cat-briers is of thorns. A boarding-house is a natural nursery of the microbes of discontent, jealousy, and gossip. Attaching it to an Institute does not change its nature. A family of fifty or sixty, all girls, is not a sedative proposition. Nor was it a tranquil job to teach four or five hundred young female minds to shoot in the direction of knowledge and wisdom. They were distracted by the flirtation-complex and the manias of school-politics. They had "crushes" on one another, and romantic "crazes" about certain good-looking boys who used to stroll slowly along the open fence of the big Institute garden on their way home from the Polymathic Academy. There were rivalries, social competitions and conspiracies, and emotional adventures which sometimes threatened danger.

Moreover there was always the alleged conflict between science and religion to make the pathway of an honest teacher, who was also an honest Christian, rough and agitated.

Anxious parents would come to Professor Wheaton with inquiries which were sometimes pathetic and sometimes angry.

"Do you think it's right to destroy my girl's faith in the Bible by letting her study this horrid stuff about Evolution?"

"Well," Wheaton would reply mildly, "you know that the theory which has been incorrectly named after the great Darwin is only a working hypothesis, after all. But all the scientific teachers are using it in their search for the truth about the actual method of creation,—a subject on which the Bible, as I understand it, was not intended to instruct us. You can't get a decent text-book on biology which doesn't make use of the evolutionary theory. If Darwin's idea is false, the only way to find it out is to study it. But if it's true, it can't possibly destroy anybody's faith in God, can it?"

"No matter! We don't want our girl to study Evolution,—not even to look at it. It will poison her mind. Her mother and grandmother were educated ladies and they got on very well without it."

"Quite so. Very well. Then your daughter should give up her course in biology and substitute a course in astronomy. That is a perfectly safe science. Even the Fundamentalists agree that we may believe that the earth is round and that it revolves around the sun, without abandoning our Christianity. Mathematics is a good safe study too. There's nothing more important for us than to know and always remember that two and two make four, not five or three. Do you see any danger to religion in that?"

Thus gently and calmly did Herschel Wheaton deal with the perturbations of fretful parents. In the same spirit he dealt with the ebullitions and occasional explosions of young female minds and with

the chronic discontent and acute complaints of boarders. Engaged in a profession which is singularly full
of troubles and small irritations, he was in fact the
calmest, most tranquil man I ever knew.

Tall, lean, muscular, full of vigorous manhood, at
forty he looked somewhat like Lincoln, but less rug-
ged in the face. Physically he was distinctly of the
Lincoln type. He had plenty of native humor in re-
serve, and all the natural passions of a man which
he kept well in hand. I suppose he sometimes went
off at a tangent in thought or feeling, but not in conduct. He was devout but not offensively pious,—certainly not pietistic. A convinced Christian of a simple kind, and a steady seeker after the truth of things
as they are, his noteworthy qualities were his unfail-
ing energy and his steady poise.

This last trait, I am sure, if not originated, was
greatly deepened and developed by his intimate and
loving friendship with the stars. This was his ruling
passion. He confessed it himself.

"I love them," he said, "not only because they are
beautiful, but because they are so steady.

'Unaffrighted by the silence round them,
Undistracted by the sights they see,'

they go on their vast ways, rejoicing, I believe, because they are obeying the infinite Wisdom and keeping the everlasting law."

"But what good can they do us? There is no practical use in studying them. They are too far away."

"That makes it all the easier to watch them and follow their motions. They are not too close to us for clear observation, like many things on this planet where we live. They have a long perspective. They are silent to our ears, yet they speak to us. As for 'practical use,' that depends on what you mean by practical. To have larger thoughts and deeper, steadier feelings,—I call that a practical use."

"But doesn't it humble you and crush you to see how many stars there are, and to think how enormous some of them must be?"

"It humbles me certainly, but it doesn't crush me at all. Why should it? We can understand them, at least in part, but there's no reason to suppose they can understand us. You remember Pascal: 'Man is but a reed, the weakest thing in nature, but he is a reed that thinks.' It's a great thing to know that you are a significant part of an immense universe."

"But don't you wonder whether any of those other stars is inhabited like the Earth? Mars, for instance?"

"Mars, my dear, is a planet. Yes, I wonder whether there are Martians. It is possible. But I do not expect we shall ever be able to prove it while we are on the Earth. One thing is sure. If any of the other planets or stars contain life it must be in an outward form absolutely different from what we know as life here. But now let us get on with our study of the Pleiades."

Thus the tranquil teacher on a clear moonless night of October, in his little working observatory, perched on a tower high above the dormant Institute, talked with his favorite pupil, Fanny Brawne. The city slumbered below them: "the very houses seemed asleep." The night lay around them like a dark-blue sea around an island. The vast constellations, the sparkling star-clusters, the long, luminous procession of the Milky Way, wheeled slowly, majestically above them. They were isolated in space. It seemed as if nothing could disturb them, no danger could come near them, lifted up as they were from the small concerns and conflicts of earth.

Yet two perils, two trials of his calm, were coming very close to Wheaton in the stillness of that circular sky-parlor. It was very bare; nothing in it but the astronomical instruments, a small table, and a couple of wooden seats; no openings, except a trap-door in the floor which led to a narrow iron stair spiralling down to the top story of the Institute, and the long aperture in the revolving dome through which the telescope peered at the slow-moving stars. There was no apparent hiding-place in that round room of twenty feet diameter. Yet danger could hide there.

Fanny Brawne was a brilliant girl of nineteen,— brilliant in every way; quick in mind, ardent in temperament, glowing in form. She was born in Louisville; but the model of her was made in Greece in the days when the Venus of Melos was fashioned. Every line of her was a curve of beauty. Every motion of her was full of vital charm. Her hair was warm brown with gold-dust in it; her forehead candid as the dawn; her eyes like star-topaz, if there be such a shining jewel; and her full red lips, innocent of paint, parted and met with an irresistible attraction in her eager talk. When she walked on the street or rode in a 'bus, men and women could not help looking at her. She was "One of Our Conquerors," as George Meredith puts it; a good girl, no doubt, but a born pirate of masculine affections.

When she saw a fine man's head she instinctively wanted his admiration to hang at her belt as a scalp.

Herschel Wheaton, her father's former protégé and chum in college, and now her tranquil teacher, was the finest man she had ever met. She admired him intensely, adored him romantically, and was curious to find out whether his calm could be shaken by a personal devotion to her. Beyond this even in her thoughts she did not go, being an honest girl. But thus far, being a woman, she went.

The work which these two persons were doing in the observatory,—verifying a diagram of the Pleiades,—brought them close together, Wheaton bending over the table, Fanny leaning above him. He could feel the warmth of her shoulder upon his, catch the fragrance of her dark hair as he breathed. Something that was not altogether calm stirred perceptibly within him. He got up from the table and went to the telescope.

"Come," he said, "look at these seven sister-stars again, and get them clear in your memory. The biggest and brightest of them is Alcyone. Three hundred and fifteen years it takes for her light to reach us. Some astronomers once thought that she was the centre of the starry universe, the point around which all the other stars are turning, making the revolution in about twenty-two million years. The smallest and dimmest one of the sisters is Merope. She has a luminous cloud about her. You can hardly see her with the naked eye. The Greeks called her 'the lost Pleiad,' because she fell in love with the mortal Sisyphus and so faded away. Fine fancies those old Greeks had!"

Fanny turned from the telescope and came very close to him, laying her hands upon his arms. Her star-like eyes spoke to him, drew him.

"Do you know," she murmured softly, "you are a very wonderful man? You are so strong, you have such big thoughts, you know so much. I care for you more than I can tell you. Wouldn't it be great if we could fly off together to one of those stars,—Alcyone, or even poor Merope? Would you care for me as I care for you?"

Wheaton was silent for a moment. Then he pulled himself up steadily and his kind gray eyes had a smile in them.

"Dear Fanny," he said, "I care for you already very much indeed. You are the daughter of my oldest friend, a beautiful girl, and my best pupil. What would you think of me if I made love to you now? You would like me less, I'm sure, and that would be very unpleasant for me. Let's not talk nonsense about flying off to Alcyone. Even if we went on the wings of light we should be more than three hundred and fifteen years old when we got to her, and she would burn us up instantly with her flaming fire. Come, it's getting late, the astronomy lesson is finished, time for you to go to bed, run along and sleep well."

Was it tears that stood in the girl's eyes for a moment? Then she smiled and held up her face to be kissed.

"Yes," she said, "you are right, my teacher. My lesson is learned. We mustn't spoil a fine thing by foolishness. Good night, and pleasant dreams."

So she went through the trap-door and down the spiral stairway,—Wheaton could hear her heels clicking on the iron steps,—and the first danger was past.

Whether his dreams were pleasant or not, no one knows. He sat for half an hour with his elbows on the table, looking out through the long aperture of the dome toward the Pleiades. But I doubt whether he saw them.

Then he took up the diagram again and worked on it till midnight. The clock on the city hall was just striking the hour when he heard a slight noise behind him and turned sharply around.

A head was coming up through the trap-door,—a shaggy head of yellow hair streaked with gray. After that came a broad, pallid face with bristling eyebrows and large pale-greenish eyes set close together. After that came a huge body of a man, almost a giant.

"This is Professor Wheaton, I believe," he said, with a slight foreign accent.

"That is my name. May I ask yours?"

"It is not known to you, but I will tell it you. My name *was* Svenson. I was born in Sweden and came to this country when I was a little boy. I have been very sick at the Long Island Hospital. I have been born again. I know *now* that my real name is John Baptist."

A slight sensation of coldness ran down Wheaton's back. He suspected that this man was probably a religious fanatic. Rather awkward to be shut up with a crazy Hercules at midnight in this lonely observatory. No bell, no telephone, no possible way of calling help. Wheaton felt that he would need to have all his wits about him. If he got excited, lost his head, who could tell what might happen?

"Glad to meet you, Mr. Baptist," he said, holding out his hand. "Won't you take a seat?"

"Not mister," replied the stranger, sitting down

A head was coming up through the trap-door. . . . After that
came a huge body of a man.

heavily, "just plain John,—a messenger of the Lord."

"Well, then, John Baptist, please tell me why you have come here at this late hour. What is it that you want?"

"I will say it in the right time. You wait and listen. I tell you first about me. I was a wild, bad man. I was sorry but could not help it. I went to church, to prayer-meeting, but no good came. The devil was in me. He would not come out. I drank much gin, ran after women, fought men. Then the great sickness came. In hospital I was strapped in bed, very crazy. Then inside me something broke. I was weak, like a baby. Then they unstrapped me. The devil was out of me. I converted. I read the Bible and prayed very much. Then I was born again, a new soul given me. I was plucked from the burning. I knew that I was John Baptist, sent to prepare the way of the Lord. You see?"

"Yes, I see what you mean. But why did you come to me? What brings you here?"

"A message from God. Listen. Glad tidings of great joy!"

The man came closer, so that the heat of his vast body was perceptible, and the faint, dead smell of

his fetid breath. His pasty face flushed a dark red.
The pupils of his eyes contracted and expanded rapidly like winking lights. His upper lip hung and
trembled as if he were about to cry. His words tumbled over one another.

"You call yourself Professor Wheaton, but I know
who you are. I heard you often pray and speak in
prayer-meeting. I followed you about the city, always meek and gentle, always doing good. You are
the best man in Brooklyn,—in the world! You are
Messiah! You are Christ come back to earth! God
sent you to save this wicked city, and I must help
you because I am John Baptist. Do you see now?"

His voice was loud and raucous. His yellowish
eyes flickered like candles in the wind. Blue flames
darted through them and they almost screamed, as a
rusty gas-jet screams when it is lighted. It was clear
to Wheaton that he was face to face with a maniac
approaching the acute stage of his delirium.

What to do? How to gain time for escape?

"Your message is a strange one. Such an idea
never entered my mind. Are you sure it's true?
How do you know?"

"I tell you it came to me right from Heaven. I
did not make it up. It came, and I know it's true."

"But how shall we prove it? How shall you and I set about saving the city?"

"By a miracle,—a miracle! a miracle! We shall push ourselves through that long window. It's narrow, but we can get through. Then we shall throw ourselves from the tower. Then"—(his face took on a look of insane rapture) "then we shall see the angels all around us. We shall feel their soft wings brushing us, their soft hands touching us, bearing us up lest our feet dash against the stones. It will be like flying, lovely, beautiful! We shall land safely on the sidewalk. All Brooklyn shall wonder, and convert to you, Messiah!"

"But how will they know about the miracle? The streets are empty now. Look, listen, no one is passing by. The people are asleep."

"The angels will wake them, and tell them, and call them. There will be crowds and crowds, I tell you. When they see us they will believe and shout hallelujah! Messiah has come! The city is saved! Glory!"

Wheaton glanced around the observatory to see if there was any weapon that he could use, any way of escape from this ghastly peril. Nothing! Before he could get to the trap-door the maniac would grab him. The iron crank for turning the telescope was too far away to reach. Without some kind of a weapon he would be helpless against those huge hairy hands like the paws of a bear, those heavy shoulders and long steel-sinewed arms. There would be a short, dreadful struggle on the floor, rolling to and fro, straining and gasping in that horrible clutch. Then the knotted fingers would close on his throat and the light would go out.

But would it? The Pleiades would still be shining. Would they not send their light into his soul, their sweet influence upon him?

"My friend," he said, "what you tell me is very unexpected, so strange that I cannot help being in doubt about it. You remember that chapter in your Bible where Christ was called to cast himself from a pinnacle of the Temple. It was the devil who tempted him, and he refused."

The lunatic sprang up and paced the floor, muttering and grinding his teeth. But his voice was weaker and lower when he spoke.

"That was different. I am no devil. I am the messenger sent before your face. You must not doubt. You must believe me. Christ did. If you are afraid, if you do not obey God's will, then I shall throw you out of that long window. You shall see what happens to the disobedient. There shall be no miracle. The angels shall not come. You shall be dashed in pieces on the stone steps."

"Very well. But will you not grant me a couple of minutes to prepare myself? I want to look once more at that little group of stars up there. I love them. They have been my friends for a long time. Perhaps God will send me another word through them."

"Friends with stars is nonsense. But I give you your way. Look at your stars if you want to."

Swinging the dome of the observatory with a touch,—it moved easily on its cannon-ball bearings, —Wheaton brought the Pleiades again into the telescopic field of vision. Serene, beautiful, dear to his heart as ever, it seemed as if they must have some gift for him, some message of calm wisdom that would be like a golden key to let him out of the prison of peril.

In a moment he knew that they had a message. He knew what it was. The first line of Horatius Bonar's lovely hymn flashed into his mind:

"*Upward where the stars are burning.*"

UPWARD—that was the key of deliverance.

He turned from the telescope and went over to the lunatic, whose fit of exaltation had abated, leaving him depressed. Wheaton laid a gentle hand upon his arm and spoke with authority.

"My friend, John Baptist," he said, "the second message has come. This is it:

"*The miracle of jumping down from the tower is too small. You and John must go down and jump up. That would be a greater miracle.*"

The crazy man's eyes were bewildered, dim, lacklustre. With the fragment of reason that was left in him, he was thinking hard, trying to puzzle the matter out.

"Yes,—yes," he said, slowly, "that would certainly be a greater miracle. Doubters couldn't say, then, that we used parachutes to come down with. They would be convinced. They would have to believe when they saw us rising to the tower. We shall do it. But not to-night. The street is bare. To-morrow noon. We want crowds and crowds to see our ascension. Come, let's go down now. I know the way."

So the strange pair descended the winding stair, Svenson ahead, and passed through the long, empty, echoing halls from story to story, and came out, at last, on the broad stone steps of the Institute.

A QUEEN'S DELIVERANCE

A QUEEN'S DELIVERANCE

THAT sacred book which is named after its heroine "Esther" is held in singular esteem and reverence by the Jews. This is not because of its religious teaching, for the name of God is not once mentioned in it; nor because of its moral value, for that is mainly negative; but probably because it records the deliverance of the chosen people from a peril in the ancient kingdom of Persia, and explains the origin of the great festival of Purim which is observed even to this day in honor of that far-off event.

Moreover it is an exceedingly well-told tale, written with great frankness and a vivid touch, and showing an intimate knowledge of human nature and of Oriental ways and manners. This makes it exciting and well worth reading by any one who is curious in these matters and has enough imagination to illustrate the story as he reads.

But beside this national tradition which has given the book a place in the Old Testament canon, there are certain outside legends which have grown up around it, and have been long current among the Persians. One of these, as it came to me through a gentleman in a black turban who was in Paris during the strife about peace in 1921, seemed of sufficient interest and moral significance to be worth writing down. So here it is.

You remember that the book of Esther begins with a story of Vashti, the first wife of the great King Ahasuerus. This same King was none other than the famous Persian monarch Xerxes, who ruled a hundred and twenty-seven provinces from India to Ethiopia, and afterward came to grief when he tried to conquer Greece.

Whatever obedience was paid to him in those provinces, (and history says that it was noteworthy,) there was one domain wherein he was not absolute, and that was his Queen Vashti.

He had made a gorgeous banquet for his princes and nobles in the palace of Shushan, a feast which lasted a hundred and eighty days. Naturally, as the banquet progressed, those who took part in it were brightly illuminated with wine, so that they forgot those reserves and restraints which are observed by good society even in the Orient. Then

Xerxes, being apparently flushed with that idiotic pride which comes with much drinking of intoxicants, sent his seven chamberlains to bid Queen Vashti come and display all her rare beauty, without regard to her modesty, before the princes and the people great and small who were assembled at the King's feast.

But the Queen was very properly holding a feast of her own with her women. This command to show herself unveiled before a throng of men was contrary to the custom wherein she had been brought up. It offended her queenly dignity as well as her womanly sense. So she refused pointblank.

Her refusal threw Xerxes into a fit of embarrassment and rage, and he sent for his wise men and said to them:

"What shall we do unto Queen Vashti according to the law?"

It may be noted that the royal despot seems to have gone somewhat in fear of his royal spouse, since he hesitated to do anything to her that was not strictly legal.

Then up spoke one of the wise men named Memucan and delivered his opinion as follows:

"Sire, this deed of the Queen is not only an injury to your Majesty; it is also an attack upon the good order of the whole realm. It will be noised abroad to all the women of Persia and Media to make them disobedient and contemptuous to their husbands. It will lead to a female revolt in which our ancient civilization will undoubtedly perish. Therefore my advice is that your Majesty should not only put away Vashti forever, but also send out a decree to all Persian and Median women both great and small, that they must absolutely obey their husbands, and that every man shall be the ruler in his own house."

So the King, greatly relieved, followed the counsel of Memucan to the letter. Vashti was ejected from the royal palace. The women in all the other palaces and houses and cottages and huts of Persia and Media were duly admonished to strict obedience.

You might think that with this the question of woman's rights in the dominion of Xerxes was ended.

But not so. For the King, apparently regretting the absence of Vashti, and following still the advice of Memucan, began to search among the virgins of Persia for one to take her place. The search was conducted by a curious method which does not particularly concern the story though it is fully narrated in the scripture. It seems to have embraced most of the beautiful maidens in the kingdom and to have been based upon a process of trial and error.

But doubtfully as we should regard this method in our days, it was apparently turned by providence, (though not so mentioned in the scripture,) to the great benefit of Xerxes.

For there was in Shushan at that time a young Jewess, as beautiful as she was virtuous, and as brave as she was beautiful. She was an orphan who had been adopted and carefully brought up by her cousin Mordecai, a Jew of excellent parts and notable adroitness. Her real name was Hadassah, which means "the myrtle," an evergreen shrub of sweet fragrance,—a pretty name to fit a pretty maid. She was in truth exceeding fair, altogether desirable, and fit for love.

The adroit Mordecai, perceiving this, managed that she should be embraced among the damsels who were gathered under charge of the chief eunuch for the King's experiment and choice. But her cousin and foster-father, knowing the law of the

Medes and Persians that the Queen must always be chosen from among the noble native houses of the country, changed the name of Hadassah to Esther, which means "a star," and much resembles the name of Ashtar, one of the favorite goddesses of the East. Thus renamed, and charged straitly by her cousin not to make known her people nor her kindred, the obedient Esther came into the King's house royal in fair raiment, having been purified six months with oil of myrrh and six months with sweet odors and other things. Her success in this primary campaign for the crown was brilliant as the rising of a star.

We know not the color of her hair nor of her eyes, nor does it greatly matter, for in these things the tastes of men differ. Endow her in your fancy with such charms as you prefer; but be sure that she had that one charm which is above all others, the will and the power to please. To this Xerxes surrendered in the first encounter. He was delighted with her to the marrow of his bones.

"By Marduk and Nebo, by Zarpaint and Ashtar, and all the divinities of Babylon," he cried in ecstasy, "this girl is sweeter than a dream and more beautiful than desire. My star, you shall rise and shine with me, and be the splendor of my house royal."

"As you will, my King," responded the pliant and supple Esther, most lovely in her meekness.

So Xerxes, deeply penetrated with love, made her his wife and Queen, and celebrated the event by a splendid feast. There is no record, however, that he bade his new Queen display her charms unveiled to the mob of banqueters. More wisely he marked the day by releasing the provinces from taxes and distributing royal largesse.

Now began a new life for the lovely and discreet young Queen, a life full of action and emotion. A plot of two rough-neck eunuchs to assassinate Xerxes, according to the custom of the country, was unearthed by the clever Mordecai. He told Esther, and she told the King in time to save his life. Haman, a pompous and purse-proud favorite of the court, having conceived a hatred of Mordecai and found out that he was a Jew, conspired and deluded the King to decree the destruction of all the people of that race throughout the realm and the spoiling of their goods. But Mordecai sent the news to his cousin Esther, persuading and encourag-

ing her, at risk of her own life to beseech the King
to revoke the decree.

"Who knoweth," said he, "whether thou art not
come to the kingdom for such a time as this?"

Esther did not know, of course. But she was
brave enough to try anything once. So she came in,
uncalled, to the King, (which was a transgression
punishable by death,) and by such arguments as a
woman may use with one who loves her, she induced him to reverse the decree. The villainy of
Haman in plotting against the Queen and her people was laid bare. He was disgraced and deposed
from all his high offices and hanged upon that very
lofty gallows which he had built for his rival Mordecai. The Jews in Shushan and throughout the
realm, being forewarned and forearmed, resisted the
myrmidons of Haman and slew them by the thousands, but laid no hand on the spoil. Thus originated the great feast called Purim, or "the casting
of the lots."

So the good and charming Queen was happy and
much beloved, not only by the doting King, but by
her country folk, and by all the people of Media
and Persia and the other lands under the sway of the
great Xerxes.

A QUEEN'S DELIVERANCE

Cousin Mordecai also prospered according to his deserts and desires. He was arrayed in royal attire, and rode upon a royal steed, and stood next to the King in all things. Xerxes being a vain and capricious monarch, exorbitant and luxurious, full of wild visions of world-wide empire, and given to that excess of wine wherein he knew not his right hand from his left nor wisdom from folly, leaned more and more upon the adroit Jew in the conduct and management of affairs. It was natural that the man whom the King delighted to honor should obtain an immense increase of riches, fame, and power.

But with this increase, whether fairly earned or due in part to his relationship to the wise young Queen, (which was of course merely an accidental consequence of his uncle's fruitful marriage in Judea,) the pride of Mordecai grew and flourished excessively. He rode abroad in state on a horse padded with cushions like a bed. When he walked, which was but rarely, the people bowed down before him. He was fed with flatteries and besieged with petitions. His house was a palace next in splendor to the abode of the King. His word was almost a law. His favoring nod was a title of distinction.

All this was of course as pleasant as the eating of sweetmeats. But it was not healthful. It brought on a severe attack of that self-complacency which is the balm of life and the bane of character.

The man who had been so admirable in adversity grew odious in prosperity. The diet of unbroken success was too rich for his blood.

To all except the King, whose temper he still feared and whom he still flattered skilfully,—to all others Mordecai was haughty and abrupt.

It was, "Here, fellow," or "There, fellow"; "Certainly not," or "Perhaps I will, if I feel like it when the time comes."

He fancied himself immensely as the architect of his own fortunes. Worse yet, he conceived the idea that he was the originator, promoter, guardian angel, practically the creator, of his glorious little cousin the Queen. For her success he secretly took the credit. Of her conduct he was inclined to take full charge. He regarded her as a mere woman, and therefore incapable of sound judgment or the management of affairs. He went back in his ideas to that ancient, disappointing dictum of the King:

"Every man shall bear rule in his own house."

Thus you see, (according to the Persian legend,

the truth of which I dare neither affirm nor deny,) the world-old question of woman's rights came up again and brought consequences.

"Is she not my daughter by adoption?" said Mordecai to himself. "Have I not trained this little Queen Esther, *née* Hadassah, and made her what she is? Her beauty is but skin deep and will wear away. But I am a wise experienced man. My judgments and counsels have enduring value. Does she not owe me obedience? She being my adopted daughter, her house is my house, in which I propose to bear rule. I will speak to her with authority. She shall follow my instructions."

The first point on which he endeavored to control her was her manner of treating her husband. As one of the family Mordecai was readily admitted to the presence of the Queen. Having been ushered in through the damask curtains by the chief eunuch, he found her Majesty busy embroidering a certain silken vest for Xerxes, whereof we shall hear later.

Mordecai began his discourse:

"Cousin," he said, "I have observed that the King does not look well. His eyes are puffy, and his hand trembles. He is too much given to the cup and the platter."

"I know it," said Esther, meekly and sadly.

"I must tell you then," continued Mordecai as a master might admonish a pupil, "that you neglect your duty toward your husband. You must warn him against these indulgences."

"I have done so," sighed Esther, "as wisely and gently as I could. By the delights of our mutual love I have sought to turn him away from those grosser pleasures."

"But that is not enough," said her Mentor. "You must be strict and stern with him. You must not plead with him. You must prohibit."

"Excuse me," said Esther with rising anger, "I will leave that for you to do. I know the King's temper better than you. Where reason and love prevail not with him, prohibition will never succeed."

"But you have the power to enforce your will," persisted Mordecai with the nasal drone of a vain weak man. "You must do as I tell you. Withdraw yourself from him until he yields."

Then Esther's eyes flashed fire and her voice had a certain ominous ring.

"That will I not do," she cried, "for then he would cease to love me. But what business is this of yours, sir meddler? Go your way! You have the Queen's permission to withdraw."

So Mordecai went out through the damask curtains, somewhat abashed. Esther continued her embroidery; but she pricked her finger and made several false stitches.

The next matter on which he sought to make his masculine will and wisdom prevail was in truth a very difficult and dangerous one, though to his imbecile conceit it seemed quite trivial and easy. It was the question of dress.

For some years the girdle of the Queen had been lengthening slightly, and very naturally, for she had borne two children. But Mordecai judged that the manner of her attire was much in fault, and conceived that it was his duty as a man of infallible taste to set it right.

"Cousin," he said, having with difficulty obtained a private audience, "I have observed that you are growing stout."

"What!" flashed the Queen, "you dare——"

"I have also observed," continued he with irritating calm authority, "that women cannot endure to hear the plain truth about fatness. Now I tell you, and I know, that you must no more wear those short garments. They make you look dumpy. You must always wear long, flowing, fringed robes."

"Hideous and awkward things," she cried, "like window-curtains. I hate them."

"Also in the matter of colors," pursued the infatuated arbiter of elegance, "your taste is bad. You shall no longer affect gay hues, but use tints more suitable, — dark purple and sober green."

"Dark purple I detest," laughed Esther, who began to see the humor of the case, "and sober green I abhor. Lilac trimmed with silver and rose broidered with gold are my favorite colors. Xerxes also admires them, and I shall wear them no matter what you say."

"You forget the deference that you owe me," persisted Mordecai. "Have I not brought you up from a child?"

"You have," she answered, smiling, "and now I am a woman. I shall please myself to please the King. You know no more of woman's dress than a camel knows of dancing. So go your way, cousin, and leave me in peace."

But when he had gone out from her presence and turned into the long dark gallery beyond, she heard a sudden noise of scuffling and violent struggle and a muffled cry of "Help, help!"

Esther ran out, fearless, and found two Persian chamberlains of the court who hated Mordecai for his rich arrogance, and who had leaped upon him in the darkness, seeking to strangle him with a noose of twisted silk. These craven murderers she buffeted fiercely with her bare hands, cutting their faces with her heavy rings.

"Begone, vile ruffians," she cried. And when they saw who it was, they fled like antelopes.

She loosed the cord from the victim's neck, and presently helped him to his feet with much tenderness, for her affection was not dead.

"Dear old cousin," she said, "have those wicked rascals hurt you?"

"Terribly," answered the trembling man. "I should have perished, but the Queen has saved my life. I am her devoted slave forever."

But this, as a matter of fact, he was not. For as soon as his strength returned, with it came back his vain dominance as a man of parts and power. He was obsessed with the desire to control Esther, and through her to direct the King.

On every occasion he corrected her, instructed

her, reproved her with his eyes even when he was afraid to speak. He vexed and oppressed her with his masterful airs. He thwarted and burdened her. He was a collar of thorns about her neck and a cloak of lead on her shoulders.

It was about this time that Xerxes meditated and prepared his gorgeous and disastrous expedition to conquer Greece. By this he intended that Asia should subjugate and rule Europe. Mordecai was hot for the enterprise in which he foresaw great profit.

"It is a noble plan," he told the Queen, "and it is your duty to encourage and urge the King to go to it."

"I think not," she answered quietly, for she had pondered the project deeply. "My opinion is right against it, for it will bring expense, sorrow, and much evil."

"Your opinion, madam," he said in a superior tone, "is neither here nor there. It is your plain duty to hearten the King in this undertaking on which he is already resolved. You must certainly do this."

"I will not," she replied firmly. "On the contrary, I shall dissuade him by all means in my power. I have received a warning from above, and have made up my mind to oppose this mad enterprise."

"Then you will sin against your father's instruction and your lord's will," said Mordecai. And he went out in a rage.

But Esther communed with her own spirit and was greatly troubled. Yet her conviction and her courage did not fail. Once again, as in former time, she faced the danger of going in to the King unbidden. So she put on her robe of rose broidered with gold and went in.

When he saw her she obtained favor in his sight, even as before, and he held out to her the golden sceptre of clemency. This she touched, and knelt at his feet.

"What wilt thou, Queen Esther?" he asked, "and what is thy request? It shall be given unto thee even to the half of the kingdom."

"My lord," she answered, "if I have found favor in your eyes, this is my humble petition: that the King should turn back from this enterprise against the Greeks who dwell beyond the sea."

"By Bel and Marduk," he laughed, "this is no humble petition. It is *more* than half the kingdom. This is a new world that I go to subdue."

"Is not my lord's dominion already very great," she replied, "and richer than any other upon the earth? Does it need increase? These Greeks are a poor people beside the Persians and the Medians and the Babylonians and the Egyptians over whom my lord rules. What profit is there in a triumph over beggars? It is not wise to wager a crown of jewels against a wreath of green leaves."

"But the land of Greece has high renown," answered Xerxes. "She boasts herself of greater wisdom than Persia. She has poets and philosophers, sculptors and painters, of whom she is proud, though she uses money of iron and dishes of earthenware. I will humble these haughty ones and make them eat out of my hand."

"Yet they are strong fighters," said the Queen anxiously, "and skilful mariners,—a hardy race. Their youths and maidens are trained to bodily vigor and prowess. They dare all for their country and know not when they are beaten."

"They shall know, when I have come to them," bragged Xerxes. "I will overwhelm them and trample them and make their poets sing my praise and their sculptors carve images of me. Dissuade me no more."

"But, my lord," said Esther trembling, "I have had warning in a dream,—a dreadful dream of a bridge swept away by a flood, and a huge ship broken on the rocks, and a mighty host scattered in defeat. Go not up against these Greeks, my lord, I beseech you by love."

"To love will I listen to-night, lovely Queen," laughed Xerxes, "but not to dissuasion. I also have been visited by a dream. Three times it came and promised me the conquest of Greece. I am surely going to my triumph. But has my Queen no smaller petition that I may grant?"

Esther thought a while before she answered.

"My request is that the King would send my cousin Mordecai to be royal governor of Paphlagonia on the shore of the Black Sea. It is a distant province, and cold, but the honor of the position will comfort him."

"I have a better thing in store for him," said Xerxes, "he shall go with me to the war and be a general in my army. Does that content my Queen?"

"It pleases me," she answered, smiling faintly, "for when he is away I shall govern the royal house here with care and bring up our children with discretion. For the rest, I am ready now to yield to the King's desire and long for his return."

So this matter was concluded, and the next day Xerxes, well satisfied, set out on his grand expedition.

Enormous was the host that followed his proud insignia. There were twelve hundred and seven huge vessels in the fleet and more than five million warriors in the unwieldy army.

Strange was the aspect of that barbaric throng advancing like a horde of locusts to devour the land. There were the Persians with their long bows and many-colored tunics protected with steel plates; the Assyrians with their brazen helmets and large clubs studded with iron; the Scythians with their long breeches and short spears; the Caspians clad in skins and carrying javelins and scimitars; the Ethiopians with their goat-horn lances and helmets made of horses' heads; the Paphlagonians with netted casques and high boots; the Thracians of Asia, with purple buskins and helmets adorned with horns of oxen; the Nysians with small leather shields and javelins hardened in the fire; and what other tribes and nations I know not, nor have time to tell.

Their commanders were bedecked with gold and

gems. They had golden and silvern vessels for their food; horses and asses for their conveyance; servants and concubines for their pleasure; carriages for the women. In a chariot drawn by Nisæan steeds rode Xerxes the Great. A bodyguard of a thousand nobles attended him. Ten thousand picked footmen, trailing spears, followed the chariot. Then came an equal number of Persian cavalry. Quarter of a mile behind them straggled a vast, disordered, and promiscuous mob.

They ate up the country like a cancer. They drank the rivers dry. To the regions which welcomed them they were a calamity. To those which resisted them they were a curse. They left behind them famine, disease, and misbegotten children.

When Xerxes looked upon his gigantic host in the plains of Abydos he wept aloud.

"Why does the Great King weep?" asked Artabanus, one of his generals who had advised against the war.

"To think that in a hundred years not one of this great multitude will be left alive."

"In less time than that," said the philosophic general, "most of these people may have perished. When we begin a thing the end is hidden from us."

Hearing with anger that the bridge he had built over the Hellespont had been destroyed by a storm, Xerxes commanded that the rebellious sea should be punished with three hundred lashes and a new bridge erected without delay. Over this the army and the camp-followers were driven with whips. Seven days and nights were spent in the crossing.

After this fashion the famous invasion of the West by the East was accomplished. But this was not the end of it.

Then followed the heroic resistance of Leonidas with his three hundred Spartans at Thermopylæ, and the costly, fruitless after-battle. The citadel of Athens was taken and burned to no purpose. The Greek fleet remained alive and ready for action at Salamis. Xerxes took his seat upon a little hill to witness the crushing of the three hundred and eighty ships of Greece by his proud armada of twelve hundred ships sweeping down from the north like a huge flock of cranes.

But the Greeks were not frogs. They were hawks. They ripped and tore and harried the vessels of the barbarians; drove them upon the shoals where they were helpless; split them asunder and sank them;

boarded them and exterminated their sailors and warriors. It was a rout, an overthrow, a marine ruin. The Persian King on his green hillside saw his glittering armada disperse and melt like snow upon the waters.

Xerxes in terror, left Mardonius, (was this Mordecai?) in command of the remnants of his army in Greece, and fled by devious ways toward Asia. Many and mean were the adventures of his flight. But at last he came to Sardis in Lydia, a rich city and full of sensual delights. Here he tarried, giving himself to the pleasures of cup and platter and to entanglements with beautiful women.

Meantime Queen Esther kept the King's house at Shushan and nourished her children. When a swift messenger came with news of Xerxes' entrance into Greece and the capture of Athens, she rejoiced. When a second messenger came to announce the disaster to the fleet and the King's flight, she wept. When a third messenger came, telling of Xerxes' sojourn in Sardis and whispering that a fair lady there, named Artaynta, boasted that he had rewarded her favors with a certain embroidered vest made for him by the Queen, Esther knew that she was free from her bonds.

So she sent another messenger, very trusty, with this letter to King Xerxes.

"Esther, once the King's wife in Shushan, to the Lord of the Medes and Persians, ruler of a hundred and seven and twenty provinces, sendeth due greeting. If ever she found favor in the King's eyes, and if now he has given the silken vest which she broidered for his body to a woman named Artaynta, then this is the petition of Esther and this her humble request of her lord. That he would grant unto her a certain house which belongs to him in Tarsus, with provision for its care, that she may live there in quietness and bring up his children in honor."

"Let her have it," said Xerxes to his treasurer. And he went on his way, sporting, fighting, drinking, dallying, until the fatal dagger provided by his son Artaxerxes let out the hot stream of his life on the floor of the seraglio.

But in the pleasant city of Tarsus, in her house by the silver Cydnus, Esther lived at peace. The lilac and the rose, the lily and the oleander bloomed in her garden. The nightingale and the thrush sang among her trees. Her son and her daughter grew beside her in strength and beauty. Her days went by as smoothly and sweetly as the river. There was no more rebellion, for she was released.

This is the end of the Persian legend concerning Queen Esther, who was first named Hadassah, that is to say Myrtle, a flower of peace.

THE DEVIL AT SEA

THE DEVIL AT SEA

THIS is a true tale of Holland in war-time. But it is not a military story. It is a story of the sea—

"The opaline, the plentiful and strong"—

likewise the perilous.

I

In the quaint Dutch village of Oudwyk, on the shore of the North Sea, lived the widow Anny Minderop with her sons. In her girlhood she had been a school-teacher, and had married Karel Minderop, the handsome skipper of a fishing-smack. Her husband was lost in a storm on the Dogger Bank; but he left her two boys, a little brick cottage, and a small sum of money invested in Dutch East India bonds. The income from these she doubled by turning her cottage into a modest tea-and-coffee house for the service of travellers by "*fiets*" or automobile, who "biked" or motored from The Hague, or Leyden, or Haarlem, to see the picturesque village with its ancient, high-shouldered church and its "*koepeltje*," commanding a wide view over the ragged dunes and the long smooth beach.

113

The tea-house, with its gaily painted door and window-shutters, was set in a tiny, exuberant garden on the edge of the sand-hills, looking out across the tulip-flooded flatlands toward Haarlem, whose huge church of St. Bavo dominated the level landscape like a mountain.

The drinkables provided by Mevrouw Minderop for her transient guests were cheering, and she had secret recipes for honey-cake and jam roly-poly of an incredible excellence. The fame of her neatness, her amiability, and her superior cookery spread abroad quietly among the *intelligentsia* in such matters. There was no publicity,—no advertising except a little placard over the garden-gate, with *WELTE-VREDEN* in gilt letters on a bright blue ground. But there was a steady trickle of patrons, and business was good enough to keep the house going.

I fell into the afternoon habit of riding out from my office in The Hague when work was slack, to have a cup of tea, a roly-poly, and perhaps a tiny glass of anisette with my pipe. These creature comforts were mildly spiced by talks with the plump widow in my stumbling Dutch, or her careful, creaking English.

She always reminded me of the epitaph,—in an

Irish church I think,—which recorded of a certain lady that "she was bland, passionate, and deeply religious, and worked beautifully in crewels." Anny Minderop was a Calvinist of the straitest sect, but distinctly of the Martha-type. She did not allow her faith in the absolute foreordination of all events to interfere with her anxious care in the baking of honey-cake and the brewing of tea and coffee.

The passionate element of her nature was centred on her two boys, who were rapidly growing to be equal to one man. He was a two-sided man. Karel, the older, was a brown-haired fleshy youth, with slow movements and a deep-rooted love of gardening. He had already found a good place with a tulip-grower in Oudwyk-Binnen. Klaas was a tow-headed, blue-eyed lad about thirteen years old, sturdy in figure, rather stolid in manner, but full of adventure. He dreamed of more exciting things than the growing of bulbs. He had the blood of old Tasman and Heemskerck in his veins. The sea had cast her spell upon him. He was determined to be a sailor, a fisherman, an explorer, a captain; and ultimately, of course, in his dreams he saw himself an admiral, or at least a rear-admiral,—a *schout-bij-nacht*, as the Dutch picturesquely call it.

"Little Mother," he would say, "didn't Holland win her glory from the sea?"

"Yes, sonny," she would answer, "but it cost her dear. Many brave Dutch bones sleep under the waters."

"What difference? It's as good sleeping under the waters as in the wormy dust of the graveyard. A man must die some time."

"But you're not a man yet. You're only a boy. It is foolish to risk losing your life before you've got it."

"I've got it already, mother. Look how big and strong I am for my age. None of the boys can throw me; and Skipper Houthof says I can tie all the sailor's knots. You don't want me to waste all that sticking bulbs in the ground and waiting for 'em to grow."

"Gardening is a good business, sonny; it was the first that God gave to man. It is safe and quiet. It is just reaping the fruit of His bounty."

"Yes, but the Bible says that they that go down to the sea in ships behold His wonders in the deep. I'd rather see one wonder than raise a million tulips. Och, mammy dear, let me be a sailor."

"But how are you going to do it? Nobody wants a boy."

"Mother dear, I'll tell you. Skipper Houthof is going to sail in his new lugger *Zeehond*, June fifth, for the herring-fishing. He's got a great crew,—those big Diepen brothers, very strong men, elders in the kirk, and the two brothers Wynkoop, and little Piet Vos, and old Steenis, and Beekman, and Groen and Bruin who always go together, and Brouwer,—those are all good Christians, you know, always go to the meeting and sing hymns. The skipper is taking young Arie Bok,—you know that nice boy in our school,—just my age,—as cabin-boy,—says he'll take me too. Won't you please let me go?"

"That would make just thirteen on the ship," said the widow, who had been counting her crochet stitches.

"Yes, but what difference? You always told me not to have these by-beliefs."

"That is right. Yet old customs sometimes have good reasons. You must let me weigh it over in my mind, Klaas; to-morrow I will tell you."

The boy went out of the room, and the widow Minderop turned to me as I sat smoking and thinking.

"It is hard to decide," she said. "Skipper Houthof is a good man, though he's young for his place. Those big Diepen brothers are fine seamen, none better; they're God-fearing men, too, though they shout too loud in meeting, and sometimes they drink too much old *Jenever* and make trouble in the village. But it isn't the captain or the crew I'm afraid of. It's the sea,—the hungry sea that took my lad's father."

"Well," I answered, "it surely is hard to decide for others; not easy even to decide for ourselves. Perhaps it is just as well that in the long run a Wiser Person decides what will happen to us. Your Klaas is a good boy, and this seems to be a good crew. When a lad is in love with the sea, you may hold him back for a while, but the only possible way to cure him is to let him try it,—and even that doesn't always work. Perhaps it ought not to. It is in God's hand,—the sea also is His."

"I believe it," she answered, "but it is a strain on my faith, when I remember——"

II

The fifth of June came around in due season. The sturdy *Zeehond*, spick and span with her new rigging, fresh paint, brown sails, nets neatly stowed under tarpaulin, rowboats on deck, lay with the rest of the herring fleet in the small stone-walled haven, easily the queen of the fleet. Flags and streamers fluttered in the light breeze; the stone walls were lined with people, chattering, singing, and shouting huzzah. As the little ships began to stir some one struck up a hymn. The loudest singers were the big Diepen brothers, tall, heavily built, masterful men. Their light gray eyes shone under heavy brows in their tanned faces, like lustrous shells in a tangle of brown seaweed. They shouted the familiar tune an octave below the key.

Some of the crowd were weeping. There is something like a wedding in the sailing of a ship; it draws tears from the sentimental.

But Anny Minderop was not crying. She wanted her eyes clear to see the last of her boy Klaas. She wanted her silk handkerchief dry to wave to him as he leaned over the *hakkebord*, looking back.

Nothing could have been more fair and promising than the departure of the herring fleet that year. It is true that the green-gray expanse of water which is called in Germany the German Ocean, and elsewhere the North Sea, is always harsh and treacherous, often covered with danger-hiding fog, and sometimes swept by insane tempests. It is true also that in the gruesome war-time the perils of the deep were increased by German submarines and floating mines. For these the cautious Captain Houthof kept a sharp lookout. But the big Diepen brothers, and under their influence the rest of the crew, recked little of these uncharted dangers. Their mind was on the fishing and the profits to follow. A typical Dutchman faces a risk calmly if there is a chance of good gain behind it.

The reports from the fishing-banks were all encouraging. The fish were already there, and coming in abundantly. They could be seen on the surface, milling around in vast circles, as if baby whirlwinds were lightly passing over the water. It was going to be a great catch for the *Zeehond*, predicted the Diepens. God was on their side, this time. He was going to make them rich if they obeyed Him.

"Even you," said the giant Simon, clapping the boy Klaas on the shoulder with a hand like a baked ham, "even you, my young one, shall carry home a pocketful of gulden to your mother, if you are good and say your prayers every day."

The boy stood as stiff as he could under the heavy caress and thanked the big man, who seemed to be really fond of him.

So far as I was able to learn afterward, the voyage went splendidly for about three weeks. Weather fair; fishing fine; eighty tons of herring; everybody working hard and cheerful. Klaas and Arie wore their fingers sore hauling and mending the nets. The salt stung them fiercely. But it was great fun. They ate like pigs and slept like logs. Simon Diepen never would let them go to sleep without saying their prayers. The tone of the lugger was a compound of fervent piety, tense work, and high good humor. Even if the other men had wanted to slacken on the piety, the Diepens would not allow it. By their bigness, their strength, and their masterful ways they bossed the ship, including the young captain. Little Piet Vos followed them like a dog. He looked on them as Apostles. The rest of the crew stood in awe, and if they sinned at all, were careful to do it out of sight and hearing of the devout giants.

With the fourth week of the voyage came a strange alteration in the luck. Weather grew cold, rough, foggy, dangerous. Fish became scarce and hard to catch. Worst of all, the gin, of which a liberal supply had been provided for daily use, gave out entirely. The Diepens, who were heavy drinkers but always steady on their legs, felt the lack more than they knew. They grew nervous, moody, quick-tempered, overbearing. They brooded over the Bible, and said there was something wrong with the *Zeehond;* God's judgment followed her for sin.

One evening in a billowing fog the lugger ran close to a mass of wreckage from some lost ship. Entangled in it were two wooden cases. The Diepens pulled them aboard, and took them down below to open them. No one dared dispute their right. They found the cases full of bottles, one of which they uncorked. It was a strange liquor, but it looked, and smelled, and tasted like dark gin. It made them feel at home. The second bottle added to this effect. The third and fourth bottles they took up to the skipper.

"Look, captain," they said very solemnly, "here is a proof that we are not yet castaways. God has warned us. Now if we repent and put away our sins, He will spare us. But we must pray hard and do His will."

Then they went below and opened another bottle. But before it was finished they fell asleep with the Bible open between them at the Book of Revelation.

In the morning gray they came on deck and Piet Vos followed them. The skipper was taking a turn at the wheel. All three of the men seemed steady on their legs, but their eyes were wild. Simon lifted up his face and began to talk with God. The skipper said he could not hear the words, but he heard the trombone voice in which God answered. Then Simon came up close, and said:

"I am Christ. God has just told me that I must clean the Devil out of this ship. He is here, in the things, in the men, especially in that damned old helmsman, Steenis. You can see the Devil looking out of his eyes."

"But what will you do?" asked the skipper. "Have a care! We must answer for everything."

"I have no care," said Simon, "but to do what God tells me. You must follow. Men will judge us, but our conscience will be clean. My brother Jan and Piet Vos heard God speak to me. The ship must be cleaned. Do not interfere, or the Devil will get you too."

Simon turned on his heel and went below. From that moment on the lugger a fatal insanity reigned and a superstitious cowardice trembled before it.

Just what happened on the doomed vessel will never be fully known. A week later a Norwegian steamship picked up the *Zeehond*, drifting helpless on the water. Three men were missing; mast and rigging, gear and boats, all gone; deck and forecastle smeared with blood; she was a gruesome floating ruin. The Norwegian towed her into Hull.

The big Diepens, Piet Vos, and two others were sent to Holland in a fast steamer. The skipper and four others were brought on a slower boat, not yet in.

The general outline of the tragedy had been printed promptly in the newspapers. But I wanted to know the particulars. What happened to the two boys? Was my blue-eyed friend Klaas safe? How had he been affected by his first adventure at sea?

III

The summer day brightened and gloomed in the sky as I wheeled along the beach toward Oudwyk and the cottage Weltevreden.

"Well contented" the name means. It is much used for houses great and small in Holland, and represents one aspect of the Dutch character. Would Mevrouw Minderop be so well contented now, after this tragedy? Or would her calm be broken, as the July afternoon threatened to break under the heavy thunder-clouds looming in the west?

After I had passed the populous bathing-station of Scheveningen the coast stretched before me in long monotony. On the right rose the dunes; steep banks and hillocks, yellowish gray on their face, crested above with rusty shrubs and tufts of wire-grass, like the wisps of hair on an old man's head. Under my wheel crunched the ashen sand of the desolate beach; bare of life, empty even of beautiful shells; tossed and tormented by the fitful wind in the dry places; corroded and wrinkled in the damp places by the waves, which advanced menacing and roaring, spread out, and then withdrew whispering, as if they conspired some day to conquer and overwhelm this low-lying, rich, obstinate land of dikes and dunes. On the left the North Sea brooded; pallid, *verdâtre*, like the rust on copper; a curious, envious, discontented sea, darkened by black cloud shadows, lit suddenly and strangely by vivid streaks of light like signals of danger, fading on the horizon into the gray mist and leaden clouds.

What wonder that the Hollanders, facing ever this menace and mystery of seeping tides and swelling billows that threaten to rob them of their hard-won land, have developed the stubborn courage, the dour pertinacity that mark their race? What wonder that on the other side, having thus far won the victory of resistance to wild waters and foreign tyrants, they are at times extravagantly merry, full of loud laughter and song, the best fighters and feasters in the world? Look at the brave gaiety of Franz Hals' *Arquebusiers*, or Van der Helst's *Banquet of the Target Company*.

When I pushed my bicycle up one of the sandy tracks that lead inland, I found myself in another, and to my eyes pleasanter, world. The sea was hidden, for the most part, by the crest of the dunes. The hills and hollows lay around me in green confusion. Mosses and trailing vines covered the ground. Clumps of pine-trees, clusters of oaks, thickets of birch and alder, were scattered here and there. Larks warbled from the sky; wrens and finches sang in the copse; rabbits scuttled into the thick bushes. It was a little wilderness, but no desert.

Presently the outlying houses of Oudwyk appeared, and at last the red gable and blue gate of Weltevreden, sitting quiet in its gay little garden. Roses and lilies, geraniums and fuchsias portioned the light into many colors by the secret alchemy of flowers. The reseda sweetened the air with its clean scent. The place was a monument of the skill and care with which man makes the best of Nature's gifts.

Within, the widow Minderop sat at her crochet-work in the tea-room. The uncertain weather had hindered other guests. She rose from her chair, dropping her work, and came to meet me with unusual eagerness.

"Yes, mynheer," she cried as if there were only one subject worthy of speech, "my Klaas is safe. God has delivered him from the sea and from those wicked men. I have a telegram from him. He is coming home to-day. Och, how I hanker to see him, to know really how he is."

A moment later the door opened and the boy came in; tanned, weather-beaten, a bit the worse for wear, but stark and sound as ever. Only his face was older, as if he had lived through years. He embraced his mother with boyish affection, saluted me with grave friendliness, and then sat down at the table to partake of coffee with unlimited honey-cakes and rolls.

At our request he began to unfold the story of his weird adventure. Reluctantly at first, and with some interruptions, (which I leave out,) he told what had happened on the lugger, and how it had struck him.

"In the beginning," he said, "it was splendid. The weather was good. The *Zeehond* is a great ship.

She rides over the waves like a water-fowl. None of them could smash her. The fishing was lucky. Everybody was in good humor. Och, mother, the sea is just wonderful. I love it.

"I don't know how long it was before the change came. The fishing petered out; the gin,—you know how much those big Diepens drink,—was all gone. They got cross and grumpy and angry at nothing. They sang and prayed more than ever; but it sounded to me as if they were not praying *to* God so much as *at* some one that they hated on the ship.

"Mother, that's an awful thing,—to hear men pray *at* people instead of *to* God! It scared me. What if God should overhear them?

"Then, after four or five days, those Diepens fished up two boxes out of the sea, and took them below. They were full of strange liquor, and Simon and Jan began to drink again, more than ever. But the drink did not make them cheerful and friendly. It made them black and sour and full of wickedness.

"Something happened on deck in the morning, before I was up. Simon told how God had spoken to him, and said that 'he was Christ our Saviour, and that there were devils in the ship, and that Simon must clean them out, by hook or by crook, no matter what it cost, no matter who got hurt. That was what our Saviour did on earth.'

"But, mother, when Christ was here many people who had devils came to Him and He *never* hurt one of them. He was kind to them. He delivered them. He made them well. That is why I was sure that it could not be the spirit of Jesus who entered into Simon. It was the big Devil himself who came in with pride and anger and strong drink.

"But Jan believed what Simon said because he was like him. And Piet Vos believed because he was Simon's little hound. And the skipper thought he had heard God's voice speaking to Simon; but he was really just plain scared because the Diepens were so big and strong and fierce. The rest of the crew were scared too, except three men. These were the ones that Simon said had devils because he hated them.

"The first was old Steenis the helmsman. He wouldn't give in to the Diepens at all. He said they were just crazy. So Jan and Simon fell on him at the wheel; cracked his head open with a belaying-pin so that the blood and brains spilled on the deck; and threw him into the sea.

"Och, mother, it was frightful. Arie Bok and I

were scared sick. But inside I was not afraid. I remembered what you told me about God taking care of us if we try to do right, and I thought that a real Hollander ought never to *show* that he's afraid anyhow.

"Why didn't we do something to stop the butchery? But what could we do? If we had stood up against those big, beastly men, they would have laughed, and snapped us in two like a pipe-stem. All we could do was to cry, and beg them to stop, and say our prayers, and keep as far as we could from the bloody work.

"The next two that were killed were Beekman and Brouwer. They were quiet men, kind of dull and stupid. But Simon said they had devils,— dumb devils, he called them. So he made them dance on the deck for about an hour to shake the devils out.

"But Simon and Jan and little Piet said the dancing was bad,—Devil-dancing, they called it; no good at all. So they drove poor old Beekman and Brouwer down below, and bashed their heads in with iron bars, and cut their breasts open with knives to let the devils loose. Then they dragged the bodies on deck, all bloody, and threw them into the sea.

While they were doing this all of them sang a hymn.

"Mother, it made me so sick, I thought I was going to die.

"The next day they set to work on the ship. They said it was poisoned by the devils and must be cleansed all over. So they cut down the mast and the rigging and threw them overboard. The rowboats, the nets, the empty barrels that stood on deck, everything was chucked into the water. Even the woodwork was hacked and broken. It made my heart bleed to see the lovely *Zeehond* abused and spoiled that way. She was so good and strong. What harm had she done?

"Then we drifted around three or four days,—I don't know how long,—like a log in the sea. We had no food except salt herrings and a few crusts of bread. But at every meal those black Diepens prayed and sang hymns and drank gin. It was filthy.

"Then a ship from Norway picked us up, and I got home somehow, I don't know just how. Och, mother, mother, I've been through hell."

The lad lost control of himself; fell on his knees beside his mother and put his head on her lap, shaken by the dry sobs of a boy ashamed to cry.

She stroked his yellow hair gently and dropped a kiss on it.

"Cry, darling," she murmured, "cry! It will do you good. You've come *through*. God has delivered you. And now you know what the sea can do to men, you'll give it up."

The boy lifted his head. His blue eyes sparkled through tears. His lips were firm again.

"Mother dear," he cried, "it was *not* the sea. It was the beastly *men*. The sea is *clean*. The sea was *kind* to us. It was vanity and hatred and drink that made the trouble. Rum and religion don't mix well. They let the big Devil into proud men. I'm going to sea again, some day. But I'll stay with you, dearest, till I grow up."

A WILFUL ANDROMEDA

A WILFUL ANDROMEDA

THE famous old Spanish playwright Calderon gives his judgment of woman—that topic about which men say so much and know so little—in a sharp couplet.

> "He is a fool who thinks by force or skill
> To turn the current of a woman's will."

I am not sure that the Don is right. At least it seems to me that his judgment is too absolute and dogmatical.

The trouble with men is that they seek either to break down a woman's will by bullying, or else to outwit it by craft and guile, deceiving her a little and flattering her a good deal. Resenting the first method, and seeing through the second, no wonder she refuses to submit. She either declares her independence by an outbreak which might almost be called an act of violence, or else she hides it by a counter-camouflage which makes you think she has yielded when in fact she had not changed her mind a bit.

But there is a third way of turning a woman's will, a *via media*, which partakes of force only in the sense

135

that reason is forceful, and of skill only in the sense
that it skilfully lets in a new light of facts on a subject that has already been too much debated in vain.
The conviction that this third way often proves good,
leads me to tell a story that I know about a girl who
once was in danger of making a mess of her life.

Of all the lovely damsels who have illuminated the
fame of Baltimore, Nancy Lang was one of the petti-
est, gayest, simplest, most romantic, and obstinate.
A fashionable finishing-school had polished but by
no means finished her. She knew everything about
the newest dance-steps, and a little, very little, about
other subjects. Her mind, lively in its motions, was
in that state where she believed all that she read in
the "*Sun* paper," (the journal which for so many
years has moulded the matutinal opinions of Baltimore). Novels of the modern Ouida type gave form
and color to her secret dreams. On the surface she
was a delightful flirt, but under the bosom of her
filmy dress she carried "a heart as soft, a heart as
kind" as that of the lover in Herrick's song. Her
flirtations were trifles. She had a half-dozen a year.
But her sentimental ideals were sacred to her, and
she was as religious as a good child.

136

This singular combination of frivolity, innocence, and devotion made her very likable; but it also exposed her to perils from designing and undesirable young men who danced in the fortnightly German at Lehman's Hall. Her father, Archibald Lang, Esq., was a strict Presbyterian elder, passing rich. His gentle Virginian wife had persuaded him to bear with Nancy's harmless frivolity; but the thought that she might be carried off by some impecunious fortune-hunter was a torment to his Scots mind. His other children were comfortably married. Nancy was his unsolved problem.

"What shall we do about her?" he asked his wife in bed one night. "It worries me; especially since that fat congressman from Louisiana has been hanging around."

"Really," she answered sleepily, "I don't know, Mr. Lang," (for she called him thus even in their most intimate moments). "You know how hard it is to change her when she takes a notion. Perhaps you might ask Sedgwick Van Allen to come down here and give us his advice."

Van Allen was the Langs' nephew, the young bachelor rector of a high-church parish in New York, strictly Anglo-catholic in his views, broad in his charities, and genial in his social relations among smart people. In fact the Langs called him, half in derision, "the worldly clergyman." But they liked his company and had confidence in his judgment on affairs of the world. For his part, he was very fond of his aunt and uncle, and still more fond of his cousins, particularly Nancy. Also he had a weakness for canvasback ducks, and terrapins, and pre-war claret. He was always a willing visitor at the Charles Street mansion.

"Now tell me, sir," said Van Allen to his uncle, as they were smoking after dinner before the marble mantelpiece in the room called by courtesy the library, "what is it that you want my advice about? Is it Nancy?"

"It is," said Mr. Lang, irritably. "That girl fair fashes me. She's soft as a kitten and stubborn as a mule. I don't know what to do with her."

"But where is the particular necessity of doing anything? She seems to me a very good girl. I can't believe she has been naughty."

"Naughty, indeed! I'd like to see a child of mine dare to be naughty! But I'll tell ye the way of it. There's a congressman from New Orleans come up here. He calls himself General Earl," (Ur-rul, Lang

pronounced it,) "but where he got the general nobody knows. He's been making up to Nancy,—old
enough to be her father,—but I'm sure the girl is
taken with him. He comes here two nights in the
week and talks with her in the parlor till I put the
lights out in the hall. He sits on the stairs at the
German and talks to her,—poetry and religion and
ideels,—oh yes, he can talk like a gramophone when
ye put the disk on. But none of my friends in New
Orleans or Washington can tell me anything deefinite
about him. All I'm sure of is that the girl thinks she
loves him."

"How did you find that out?"

"She confessed it. I told her that he had never
asked me permission to pay his addresses, and that
he was too old for her, and that he was not able to
support her, and that he was a gas-bag. Then she
began to cry and said he was her ideel. Then I
told her I'd forbid him the house, and she cried
more."

"But, my dear uncle, they could meet in Druid
Hill Park where Nancy walks or rides every day.
You can't have a detective to follow her around and
keep this invading general off."

"Perhaps not. But I can make the girl understand

what I told her, that he shall not hang up his hat in my house."

"What did she say?"

"She only cried more. Then she went up to bed, and as she went out she said something about 'going to him.' Now what do you think of that?"

"It looks a bit dangerous, but I don't believe it's final. You see I have never met this general."

"No, and ye don't need to,—the crafty gold-digger, the swaggering reaver of other men's lambs. But tell me, you that are so wise in the world, how will I get rid of him? How will I break the girl's will?"

"That would be a hard job, I'm afraid. You see she's *your* daughter."

"That she is. And for that reason she must mind what I say. This man must be dropped. She's fair silly about him,—a man of no standing and no business except politics! She must be daft to think of him. I'll break it off short. I'll disinherit her."

"But that might lead to something very unpleasant, an elopement, a family quarrel. You know how you would hate to see it all in the newspapers,—with snap-shots of the principal parties. You remember what happened to Cabot Winslow last summer,—

two daughters most carefully brought up,—one ran off with the electrician, the other with the chauffeur. The old gentleman was so shocked and mortified that he wouldn't go to his club for three months. And in the end he will have to surrender. The only advice I can give for the present is not to do anything hasty or harsh. After all Nancy loves you. Let me have time to think over the affair, and meet this general, and get some lines on him. There must be a way out, though I can't see now what it will be. Meantime let's sleep on it. *La nuit porte conseil.*"

The next morning Van Allen came down rather late to breakfast, and Nancy was there most charmingly to pour coffee for him. She looked at him with demure eyes.

"You and father were up late last night."

"Yes, we had a lot to talk about,—politics, and society, and the church,—all sorts of things."

"And me?"

"Well, yes, your name was mentioned several times, if I remember rightly."

"You bet it was. You know you can't fool me. That was the point of the whole play."

The girl's eyes flashed, and her lips took on that *mutine* curl which made them so fascinating. Then she pulled a chair over beside him and put her arm over his shoulder, greatly to the hindrance of his business of eating an egg, English fashion, out of the shell. She pulled out the flute-stop in her voice.

"Dearest Sedgy, you're not going to be against your fond little cousin in this thing, are you? It's breaking my heart. General Earl is so fine, so noble, —just the greatest man I ever knew well. But father is so unreasonable, so hard, almost cruel sometimes, —though I love him as much as ever. But he can't expect me to give up my ideal just because he orders me, can he? You're *not* going to be against me, *are* you? I'm so unhappy."

No man can be expected to blurt out the entire truth under conditions like that. So Van Allen took her left hand in his and squeezed it and told part of the truth.

"Nan darling, you know I never could be against you. I'm really *for* you all the time. Your father must put up a better reason than 'orders' if he wants you to give up your ideal. It isn't done nowadays, —indeed it never was truly done that way. But look here,—I have an idea! Why not come to New York with me on the ten o'clock? You have never seen my rectory yet. Aunt Sabrina Sedgwick is keeping

142

"It's breaking my heart. General Earl is so fine, so noble,—
just the greatest man I ever knew well."

house for me. She'd be delighted to have you and so would I. Come along. Run up like a blue streak and pack your bag. You'll only need one dinner-dress."

The girl jumped up and clapped her hands.

"Old thing," she cried, "you're absolutely great! How did you ever think of it? But—" (here she hesitated, looking at him shyly)—"but could I,—could I,—well, could I see my friends there? Suppose, f'rinstance, General Earl should come to New York. Could he,—could he,—well, you know,—could he call on me?"

Van Allen suppressed a smile.

"Sure," he said, "not only call, but be asked to dinner. Don't forget to put that in your telegram. I'll make this visit all right with your mother. Speed up now on that bag or we shall be late."

The telegram was sent, the easy journey made, the rectory reached in time for a late luncheon. Aunt Sabrina,—a Sedgwick of Stockbridge, if you please, representative of New England's blue blood, wise, witty, and full of Victorian formalities which she called principles,—was instantly captivated by Nancy and received her warmly. General Earl called at five o'clock, saw Nancy alone, (having forgotten to send up a card for her aunt), and was invited to dinner at eight o'clock.

When he appeared Van Allen's fears were confirmed. The general was a dark pudgy man, with a fat upper lip adorned by a short bristling mustache, and a bald place on top of his head which he partly concealed by letting his hair grow long on one side and brushing it over to the other side. He wore a dinner-coat, gray waistcoat with white mother-of-pearl buttons, and a white satin necktie. His manner was that of a colored head waiter in a Saratoga hotel,—florid. But he could talk,—and he did, to an excruciating degree.

"Will you have a glass of wine with me?" asked Van Allen as the *entrée* was served. "My father brought it over long before the war,—Château La Rose 1904,—so Mr. Volstead's ban does not affect it."

"Sir," said the general, "I never drink wine. I regard it as a reprehensible and dangerous habit. Wine, sir, in any form is a virulent poison. You recall what Shakespeare said about it." (Then he declaimed the well-known speech of Cassio.) "It is a treacherous friend and a subtle foe. It is the main cause of all the misery in the world. The greatest

144

thing a man can do to relieve the sufferings of humanity is to abandon, nay to prohibit the use of wine absolutely. Mahomet was wise and humane when he forbade his followers to partake of the fomented juice of the grape. I hope you agree with me, sir."

The host could not say anything; Nancy listened with adoring eyes; Miss Sabrina, whose face expressed first astonishment, and then one of her Victorian formalities, put an icy question to the speaker.

"Do you regard the Turks as especially noble and humane, and Mahomet as wiser than our Lord?"

"Madam," said the general, "you will pardon me for saying that your interrogatory is without application or pertinence to the question we are now discussing. It is not a question bearing on or appertaining to the grea-a-at crusade by which the human race is to be led into the Golden Age. Yes, sir,—yes, ladies,—the grea-a-at New Era so long foretold by prophet and bard is now upon us. The suffering race of mankind,—I mean, of course, the noble white race, divinely chosen to rule and govern the world,—under the leadership of men of vision and courage, will shake off the timid trammels which have been imposed upon it by leaders falsely so called,—I mean, of course, churchmen, and physicians, and financiers,

—and leaping responsively to the call of that eloquence which speaks directly to the heart of the mass of mankind,—I mean, of course, the mass of the heart of mankind,—will press forward to an era of universal health, wealth, and happiness."

Nancy's face shone with admiration; Miss Sabrina's eyes sparkled with restrained Yankee common sense; Van Allen trifled with his salad and put a polite question.

"How do you intend to accomplish this great result?"

"By legislation, sir," replied the general, "by courageous, forward-looking, all-embracing legislation which shall regulate every detail of human life from birth to burial. A Congress freely chosen by the noble white race of America shall mark out the path wherein all the people must walk. No babe shall enter the world without congressional license; no defunct citizen shall be laid in the tomb otherwise than as Congress may decree. Everything,—food, beverages, medicine, education, marriage, every human function,—shall be congressionally controlled. Thus shall America very wonderfully become the home of the free and the land of the brave. Thus shall she, this grea-a-at democracy, standing aloof in gorgeous insulation from the old world with its rivalries and prejudices, shaking off the trammels of history, which is bunk, and the fallacies of economics, which were invented by bankers, set a glorious pace of progress for all humanity and deliver the world from the cancers which are now fanning the whirlwinds which are at present digging our graves."

Here the general, slightly out of breath, paused for a moment, and wiped his fat upper lip with his handkerchief, while Nancy gazed on him in a trance of fascination, Miss Sabrina's head shook so that her tiny lace cap trembled, and Van Allen concentrated his attention on cracking a walnut.

"Do not imagine, sir," continued the general, having caught his second wind as if from one of the whirlwinds he had mentioned, "do not hypothecate that I am opposed to everything that is old,—churches, universities, learned societies. But these things must be regulated and controlled by Congress, the *fontanus et origens* of the people's wisdom and power. Nothing must be taught without congressional sanctum. Nothing must be held sacred without its *imponentur*. This will give uniformity to liberty, and clothe the action of the individual with the ægis of legislative authority. We must make a new world for the new era. Take that ancient institution which you, sir, represent so well. The church,—what is it now but a dusty congeries of moth-eaten rites and cerements, a voice telling fairy-tales in the wilderness? I do not say it must be abolished, for we can still use it for our purposes,—to elect uplifters to Congress and to compliment their legislation with the sanctums of religion. But I say without hesitation that if the church is to be worth what it costs in exemption from taxes, we must have a brand-new Christianity, something big and buoyant and belligerently pacifist. It must get rid of all this stuff about penitence, and cross-bearing, and humility, and brotherly love. Brotherly justice is what we want. What happened down in Judea makes no difference. One hundred per cent American legislation is what the world needs to-day to bring in the Age of Gold."

By this time Van Allen had succeeded in catching his aunt's eye, which was growing rather wild. She rose and nodded to Nancy, who was still entranced by the general's eloquence. The rector stood up and opened the door for them; the two ladies went to the drawing-room, the elder marching like an indignant little grenadier, the younger glancing back with soft reluctance. The men remained to smoke that fragrant Indian weed which is supposed to soothe the nerves and promote digestion with good humor. At least that was Van Allen's intention as he offered the general a mild, well-seasoned Corona.

"Tobacco, sir," said the irrepressible one, tipping back in his chair and waving his pudgy forefinger to enforce his remarks, "tobacco next to alcohol is one of the greatest curses of the human race. The man who uses it in any form is committing suicide. I never use it."

"It is a pity," said Van Allen slowly as he lit his cigar with care,—pausing slightly between the puffs, —"because your friends the Turks seem to be rather fond of it."

"That, sir, is a defect of ignorance. They have not yet attained to that degree of scientific knowledge which is common among the plain people of America. We know, sir, that the juice of tobacco, which I may tell you is called nicotine, is a deadly and persuasive poison. It penetrates all the tissues of the body, the nerves, the muscles, the sinews, the flesh, even the bones. Yes, sir, post-morbid examination has revealed the relaxing presence of nicotine in the bones of confirmed smokers. Think of that, sir!"

"Do you happen to know whether this relaxing

presence has been observed in the bones of the skull?"

"Certainly, beyond a doubt it has. It must have been. You have probably noticed that smokers are loose thinkers, vague, incoherent. That is because the bones of the head are relaxed. Only those who abstain from tobacco have perfectly solid heads."

"That is a very, very serious thought," said Van Allen tossing the remainder of his cigar into the open fire. "I believe it will come back to me after many, many days. Then I shall thank you for bringing it to my attention. And now shall we join the ladies?"

Miss Sabrina was in the back drawing-room softly playing over some of Mendelssohn's "Songs Without Words" on an old-fashioned grand piano. Nancy was in the front drawing-room seated in an S-shaped tête-à-tête chair built for two. Evidently she awaited the general, who promptly sat down opposite her, and dived plump into the depths of a profound conversation. Van Allen lingered for a moment by the piano, and then excused himself on the plea of having some work to do for the coming Sunday.

But when he got into his den, where a pleasant fire of logs was burning on the hearth, he did not turn to his books or his pen. He lit a big pipe and gave himself up to thoughts which were apparently not altogether happy. After a while Miss Sabrina knocked lightly at the door and came in without waiting for an answer. She perched on the edge of the sofa.

"My dear boy," she cried, "did you ever see such a—really I can't describe him,—such a flamboyant bumpkin, such an embroidered gunny-bag? Really an insufferable person, quite beyond words. How can that lovely cousin of yours be taken with him? Every word he said trod on your toes. How can Nancy stand him?"

"Love, my dearest aunt, laughs at manners, as well as at locksmiths."

"But you must do something to stop this infatuation. She is like a pretty little bird fascinated by a fat boa-constrictor. You must save her, do something to break it off."

"But how?"

"You can find out something discreditable about him, I'm sure. I don't believe he is such a paragon of all the virtues as he pretends to be. You can uncover some dark places in his record if you look it up."

"Even so, Nancy might not believe in them. She

might say his enemies invented them. And if she did believe, she might cling to him all the closer on that account. Ministering angel, you know,—help him to redeem his past in the glorious future to which he is dedicated. A girl revels in that rôle. It sets her up."

"You're too cynical, Sedgwick. It's a bad fault in a clergyman. Nancy is such a darling. I'm certain the man is an adventurer, too—a fortune-hunter. He probably has no property and no business to speak of. Show him up to Nancy."

"If I did she would probably think I was showing him off. Noble adventurer, despises money! Poverty shared with him would be bliss."

"You take this thing too lightly, nephew. If she marries him she'll be wretched. He won't wear well, —shoddy stuff! If she quarrels with her father there will be a great misery, a broken heart, perhaps two. His will is hard as nails, and hers, under all her pretty softness, is hard as—well, as tacks. Something must be done, and very soon, before this silly affair goes too far."

"I know it, auntie; and the affair is not really silly, it's terribly serious. There is probably only one way out of it, and I don't know whether I can find that. But I will do my best, my very best, I promise you. You must be satisfied with that."

So they said good night. Half an hour later Nancy tapped lightly at the study door, and came in with radiant face.

"Oh," she cried, "I've had the most wonderful talk—simply thrilling! He's gone now, had to take the midnight train for Washington, congressional duties. He has the strongest sense of duty, you know. Don't you admire him, Cousin Sedgy? I knew you would. Isn't he simply wonderful?"

"He is certainly a remarkable man," said Van Allen, gravely smiling.

"I was sure you would see it, you are so clever. Do you wonder I l-like him more than any man I ever met? He has such great, noble ideas. How long am I to stay here, Sedgy dearest?"

"As long as you like, little Nancy. Certainly over Sunday, that is four days. Perhaps I may have to go to Washington on Monday, then I can take you with me in my new car and leave you at Baltimore."

So the girl went to bed contented, but wondering about the reason for her cousin's possible trip to Washington. It was connected, in fact, with some letters of discreet inquiry that he had written to friends of his at the capital in regard to General Earl. The letters suggested, without definitely saying so, that the eminent statesman had approached the influential clergyman with reference to certain schemes of benevolence. These he was not at liberty to describe at present, but of course he wished to know as much as possible about the promoter.

The answers were prompt but not very illuminating. The general was an undistinguished congressman of copious oratorical gifts. He was supposed to be a lawyer, but had no business except politics. He had been involved in a scandal about the harbor improvements at New Orleans some years ago, but a friendly judge had cleared him. He had changed his party twice, and was not on any committee of the House. His seat was not regarded as very secure. His habits, so far as known, were regular. Men did not like him much, but he seemed very popular with the ladies. One old-fashioned letter called him "a bald-headed beau"; another, more modern, called him "a fat old philanderer."

"Nothing here," said Van Allen, "that would have the slightest effect on that darling little idiot Nancy. She would say it was all envious gossip."

But on Saturday a note came from Mrs. Schuyler Wendell, a parishioner and great friend of his, who was spending the Spring with her daughter Cristina in her apartment on Connecticut Avenue. Yes, she knew General Earl quite well, through her Cristina; and she wished very much that her dear rector would come down and make them a visit as soon as convenient.

At this point the worldly clergyman thought he saw a ray of light on the way of deliverance. "I knew it," he said to himself in honest glee, "that fat upper lip made me sure of it."

On the Monday he made the southward journey in his swift shining roadster with Nancy, left her at her father's door in Charles Street, and went on to Washington, where he was welcomed with evident pleasure by Mrs. Wendell, and with friendly raillery by the handsome, clear-eyed Cristina; a tall, shapely young woman of about twenty-five.

"What brings your reverence here?" she asked. "Lobbying?"

"Not exactly," he answered. "It is a combination of business and pleasure. My first purpose was to see your mother. I knew you would not let me do that without seeing you,—an added pleasure. My second purpose has a slight connection with Congress, I admit."

"Well then," she said, "since you are so stuck on mother you shall have her all the evening to yourself. I am going to a dinner-dance."

"With the nobility, no doubt," he mocked. "But will you promise to go out with me to-morrow in my little car? It is a beauty. You shall drive,—though I hear you break speed-laws as recklessly as hearts."

"Righto," she laughed, "they were made for that. I'll drive you, since you won't be led. But if you fancy I don't know already that you have a pastoral lecture in store for me, you've got another guess coming to you, that's all. Till to-morrow, reverend sir!"

The little dinner for two in the apartment was delightful: soft lights, no music, suave air coming in at the open windows laden with the delicate fragrance of Spring flowers, and conversation which ranged far on light wings, and was alive with that quick mutual understanding which can leave many things unspoken. Mrs. Wendell was an "elect lady" like the one described in the New Testament, (see II John,) and her interest in the church was unfeigned and practical. She wanted to know all about the Sunday-School, and the Poor Fund, and the Summer Camp for Working Girls, (to which she promised a generous subscription,) and the Evening Classes for Men, and the Seaside Rest for Tired Mothers, and all the working functions of a modern city parish. The rector told her all the news concisely, and she commented on it with wit and sympathy. Then, after the table was cleared and the chairs were moved to the window where the smoke of Van Allen's cigar floated out into the blue, she came to the point,—like a woman, —very directly, after fetching a long compass round.

"I sent for you, my dear rector, to consult you about Cristina. I'm rather worried in regard to her."

"Nothing serious, I hope. She's looking splendid. There can't be anything wrong, I'm sure."

"No, I don't believe there is anything serious, but it's very annoying. There is a man named Earl,— a congressman of the garden type,—a quite undesirable person from my point of view, but an eloquent talker,—he has been devoted to her for three months. He is what we used to call in Victorian days, her 'suitor.' In old times one could have suppressed him, simply forbidden him the house. But nowadays that doesn't go. You know what modern girls are, and I don't object to it at all, if they will only use discretion. But this Earl person is rather impossible.

He seems to be absolutely infatuated. He makes himself conspicuous, and Cristina,—well, I can't believe she is in love with him, but she lets him go on. When I speak about it she laughs. He writes to her and even telegraphs to her constantly. He walks with her two or three times a week, and sits out dances with her in the conservatory. The affair is being talked about, I was afraid you might have heard of it in New York. This man has certainly made an impression on her, though it may not be deep. I don't like him. I don't trust him. He looks to me like a designing person. What shall I do about him?"

"Nothing, dear lady, absolutely nothing, provided you will trust me and persuade Cristina to do the same. The Lord has delivered this Philistine general into our hands."

Then he told her about Nancy Lang in Baltimore, —her prettiness, her young innocence, her gaiety, her idealism, her stubborn will, her obstinate devotion to the fat-lipped one.

"And this, you see," he added, "is really a serious affair. Cristina's is only an episode in the education of a princess. But my little cousin Nancy is caught, and can't get out. There is only one way to deliver her from this fellow's spell. Will you ask Cristina to let me see all the general's letters and telegrams to her?"

"I will indeed," Mrs. Wendell answered, "and I'm sure Crissie will do it. She has always liked and trusted you, though she sometimes speaks to you so disrespectfully. I hope you don't mind."

"I simply love it," said the rector, with emphasis.

Next morning Miss Wendell carried a neat gray leather despatch-case as she got into the two-seater with Van Allen and took the wheel. She looked beautifully efficient as she steered the car among the blooming squares and circles which make the streets of Washington seem like an intermittent park. The soft gray of her dress, her hat, her gloves, the veil over her ears and round her neck, gave the fine rose of her face a perfect setting and deepened the color of her eyes to the purple of a pansy. Her companion talked to her a little, just to excuse his looking at her so much. But she kept her eyes on the road and her hands on the wheel.

When they came to the Baltimore highway and saw it clear before them, she let the car out to the limit. It was almost like flying,—a smooth, breathless, gently purring rush through a world of tasselled and embroidered green, flooded with clear joy of sunshine. Every cottage garden was aglow with tulips and daffodils, and the hedges of forsythia seemed woven of warm gold. At last the girl was satiated with speed. She relaxed the pressure of her foot on the pedal, and leaned back in her seat.

"Some car!" she said, smiling. "Oh, by the way, I brought those foreign despatches mother said you wanted to see."

She passed the small gray satchel over to him with her left hand.

"Thank you, Cristina," he said as he took it. "You are fine to do this; it means a great deal. I suppose your mother told you the whole story?"

"Yes, she did, and I don't care to hear it again. Poor little cousin Nancy! I'm sorry for her. What are you going to do with this rubbish? Show it to her, I suppose."

"That is what I intended, with your permission."

"Isn't it rather treacherous to show private letters?"

"Usually, but you know you can't be treacherous to a traitor."

"Right. The man is a stupid old beast. I should

hate him if I didn't despise him. I never want to see him or hear his name again. Do what you like with that stuff. But do you know you are going to break your pretty cousin's heart?"

"I think not. She has too much pride for that. I mean to save this little Andromeda from the dragon, even against her will. You remember that verse in the Psalms about 'deliver my darling from the power of the dog'? That is what I mean to do, and this is the only way that I can see to do it."

"Gallant chevalier!" said Cristina, (but there was no mockery in her eyes now). "I guess you would dare anything for her sake, wouldn't you? Perhaps she will reward you some day later, when she gets over her hurt,—a wreath of grateful love to her deliverer?"

"Please don't talk nonsense," answered Van Allen, looking straight into the amethystine eyes. "I want nothing at all but to get that wilful Nancy out of the dragon's power, and to keep your,—your friendship,—whatever you can give me!"

"Your chances seem to me good," laughed the girl, "that is if you behave nicely,—I don't mean what you call nicely,—I mean what I call nicely. Now we must hurry home to lunch. You can drive going back if you like. Step on the gas, or we'll be late and mother will scold."

It was half past four in the afternoon when the roadster drew up at the marble steps of the Charles Street mansion. Van Allen asked to see "Miss Nancy, alone, in the drawing-room, please, and if any one else calls, Stephen, you can say she is not receiving to-day." The white-haired negro butler bowed and smiled. He understood perfectly, or thought he did,—which amounted to the same thing.

When the girl came down she looked pale and worn. There had been a sharp scene at dinner the night before. Her father had made fun of her "ideal"; she had replied stubbornly: he had stated his commands emphatically: she had left the table in tears, and spent a sleepless night,—at least she thought it was sleepless,—which amounted to the same thing. The chevalier approached his difficult task with reluctance.

"Nancy, I have just been in Washington."

"I know that, stupid. What did you go for?"

"To see some old friends of mine: Mrs. Wendell and her daughter Cristina."

"Is she pretty?"

"Some people think so. General Earl, for one,

must think so, because he has been making love to her desperately for the last three months. I hate to have to tell you this, but it is a thing you ought to know."

"I don't believe you. You are just lying about him."

"That is a hard word, cousin, but never mind it. I don't expect you to believe me. I have brought you the proofs."

"What on earth do you mean?"

"Miss Wendell has kindly let me have the letters and messages that the general sent to her. Here they are for you to read."

"She is a mean old cat. I don't want to see them."

"Whatever she may be, she is not that, I assure you. She is a fine girl, just as proud and honorable as you are. You may say that you do not want to see the letters, but in your heart I know you do. In fact it is your duty to see them, and to read them carefully."

"Did you tell that girl about me?"

"I did not," he answered, hedging a little, "for some one else had already told her. So she thought you ought to know about the letters."

"She wants to get him for herself, that's it."

"On the contrary, she despises him and naturally, too. She will never speak to him again,—said so in very strong language. She has a lot of pride. He would not dare to face her."

"Well, then," said Nancy, rather pitifully, "what do you tell me to do, Mr. Inquisitor?"

"I don't tell you to do anything, dear, except what your heart tells you to do. If you want my advice, it is very simple. Take these letters and telegrams with you where you will not be disturbed. Read them side by side with those which you undoubtedly have locked up in your desk. Then make up your mind whether you think the writer is worthy of such a precious thing as your love. No one can force you to give him up. I will stand by you through everything. Please do not try to come down to dinner tonight. You will have a headache, and you can ask to have something sent up to your room. When you want to see me, after you have made up your mind, let me know. Will you, Nancy?"

She nodded, with wet eyes, and went off carrying the fateful, (and hateful,) gray satchel. Van Allen stood looking after her. Though it was not the custom of his church, he murmured an extempore prayer. "Lord, help this dear child to a proud spirit!"

The dinner that night was dull and awkward. Not even the diamond-back terrapin and the vintage of the *Côte d'Or* 1898 could enliven it. Mr. Lang was inquisitive about the visit to Washington; but Van Allen sidestepped the inquiries by declaring that, really, he had no news to tell,—it was only a visit to old friends and parishioners. Later in the evening, finding that the marble mantelpiece got on his nerves, and the postprandial cigar was too strong, he went out with his pipe in the moonlight, to walk around Mt. Vernon Square, where Barye's bronze lion sits on its haunches hungrily waiting for G. Washington, Esq., to come down from his tall white monument. When the rector got back to the house in Charles Street the snowy-haired butler welcomed him with a confidential whisper.

"Miss Nancy, suh, she say please infawm reverend she waitin' faw him in her boodore, yes suh. Please rest yo' hat, suh."

When he entered the friendly room he found his cousin somewhat dishevelled but still very lovely.

Her eyelids were slightly swollen, her hair in disorder, but there was a bright red spot in each cheek, and a dancing light in her eyes. She sat at her table, which was covered with papers.

"Oh, Sedgy," she cried, "do come here and look! This is perfectly horrible and ridiculous. That old fraud has been writing and telegraphing to her from Baltimore and to me from Washington,—on alternate days, mind you! See here."

There were the *pièces justificatives* of the general's bold perfidy and plentiful lack of originality. Those on yellow paper were restrained as telegrams must be. They spoke in symbolic language. For example, "Washington, March 12. To Miss Nancy Lang. Detained by business. Dull weather here. Hope sun will shine tomorrow on Eutaw Place by four o'clock. Leander." "Baltimore, March 13. To Miss Cristina Wendell. Kept here by business. Weather dreary. Hope sun will be bright in Dupont Circle tomorrow by five o'clock. Leander."

The letters, on pink paper, scented, and surmounted with an earl's coronet, were frankly and floridly amorous. They bubbled with protestations, endearments, fond petitions, usually quite varied. But sometimes invention seemed to flag, and a letter to the Washington address looked like the twin of one that had been sent to Baltimore. Here is a condensed example.

"Most lovely and adored Nancy (Cristina):

"In this desert of Washington, (Baltimore,) the thought of you is the oasis of my soul. The light of your brown (blue,) eyes, brighter than topaz, (sapphire,) is the starry jewel of my sad, strong heart. I have never seen a woman so resplendent, so fairylike, (queenly,) as you. You control me as the stars guide destiny, (moon rules the tide). The only hope of my existence is to make thee mine, as I am

THINE ADORING EARL."

As Nancy read this astonishing two-faced revelation of a single soul, she laughed a little and wept a little.

"O pig!" she cried, "fat, deceiving, double-dyed pig! How did you ever get me to believe in you? Sedgy dear, I've m—m—made," (sobs here,) "a d—d—darned little fool of myself. What shall I do now?"

He put his arm around her shoulder and patted her gently.

"Cry it out, old girl, and then forget it. You're young and full of courage. Many a girl makes a fool of herself and doesn't know it till too late. Anyhow, making a fool of yourself is much better than if God had spared you the trouble by making you one at the start."

"But what shall I do now? I'd like to box that old wretch's ears and give him a piece of my mind!"

"Why waste good material? All you need to do is to make a bundle of this silly stuff, both sections, and send it by post to Mr. Earl, without note or comment. He'll recognize his own effusions and know that the game is up."

"Don't I need to do anything more? Oh! I feel so happy, just as Andromeda must have felt when Perseus cut her loose from that horrid rock. Can't I show it some way?"

"Well, to-morrow morning when the sun is bright on Dupont Circle and Eutaw Place and Charles Street too, you might tell your father that you're sorry you made such a d—d—darned fool of yourself, and that it's all right now, and that you are anxious to embrace him if properly invited."

"I'll do it, sure. Anything else?"

"Only one thing. In cases like this it is customary

for Andromeda, if not too angry, to kiss her un-
worthy rescuer good night."

Here the curtain-raiser ends and the play begins.
You can guess for yourself how it continues.

No, Nancy does not marry her cousin, but a brilliant young surgeon of Johns Hopkins Hospital, to
whom she makes an admirable wife. It requires two
bishops and an archdeacon fitly to perform the nup-
tials of Cristina Wendell and the Reverend Sedgwick
Van Allen in St. John's Cathedral, despite which
pomp and circumstance they are absolutely happy.
The doughty General Earl is retired from public service without a pension or a wealthy wife. When last
seen he is in Montana, ardently pursuing a Miss
Arabella Clutch, red-haired and only daughter of a
Copper Senator.

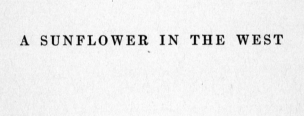

A SUNFLOWER IN THE WEST

A SUNFLOWER IN THE WEST

THE vast oval valley of Jackson's Hole, rimmed with mountain ranges, flushed with the golden light of a September afternoon, was like a cup of jade filled with yellow wine. But in the gradual advance of evening it seemed as if the cup were slowly tilting toward the east, the warm radiance spilling out over the Grosventre hills, the cold shadow seeping in from the base of the Giant Tetons, till presently the gold would be all gone and the gray would fill the beaker.

The man who was riding through the sage-brush across the ancient lake-bed toward that curious projection called the Timbered Island,—a dark ridge of forest rising abruptly from the pale sea of bluish-green bushes,—felt that the shadowing of the valley was somehow like a process that was going on in his life. I do not mean the inevitable progress of the years and the gathering dusk of old age. That had not yet made itself known in his experience. In his fiftieth year Leroy Macrae was still hale and hearty, sound in body and mind, with a good appetite for the joy of living. But something within his spirit was ebbing away, fading out, leaving the world darker and duller around him.

"Might as well face it," he said to himself, "I'm growing aged as well as old. I've crossed the divide. Now the trail runs down-hill into a dim country,—dismal prospect,—chilly! People think me a successful man; but I know I'm really a failure. Done some good work: got high wages: but no reward to make it all worth while."

Now Macrae is not the hero of this story; but he plays a decisive part in it; and in order to understand it and read the meaning of its title, you must know a little more about him.

He was what Goethe calls a "problematic nature," —a blend of opposites. A Kentucky boy, adventurous, dreamy, imaginative, fond of music and poetry, he was gifted, (or handicapped, as you choose to put it,) with a keen mind, great power of application, and extraordinary practical efficiency. He loved his violin, his Shelley, and his Keats. But his university studies, however tough they were, had an attraction for him and he mastered them. Their very toughness was a challenge to his manhood.

When he took up modern chemistry with its

mysteries of atoms and molecules and fluent elements and strange combinations, it fascinated both sides of his nature, his imagination, and his love of doing things. He was so successful in this branch of science that he made a young renown and won a professor's chair at Calvinton University. Therein he sat contented for a few years, pursuing his researches, teaching his pupils, discoursing mystically of "the personality of compounds," and inventing new ones. He also played liberally on the violin, composed ballades and lyrics, and paid harmless rotary court to several lovely ladies,—until the idea struck him that he ought to get married. He did. And by this act his path was turned, marked, and fenced in.

Olivia Barr was what is known as an awfully pretty girl. Under her golden hair and behind her bright blue eyes she had a firm female mind, not large but very set. She had been well brought up and taught to believe that the things she admired were necessarily admirable and that her modes of conduct were the best if not the only ones. Her ideas of religion were limited to the practices of St. Petronius' Church. Her notions of human intercourse were confined to the customs and manners of her

own social set. She scorned anything Bohemian.
She was one of those women who keep all the ten
commandments but never have a generous im-
pulse.

Macrae's cleverness and efficiency impressed her;
his stalwart good looks attracted her strongly; she
accepted him as an important aid to her fixed plan
of life, into which she moulded him by her mild per-
sistence, for he was really a peaceable man. She
made him dissatisfied with a professor's small sal-
ary and intangible reward; focussed his attention
on the cash profits of commercial chemistry; and
by skilful efforts landed him in the rich berth of
Chemical Director and second Vice-President of the
immense Dufour Corporation. Here he toiled,
shrivelled, and grew wealthy, inventing dyestuffs,
high explosives, and poison gases, which he hated.
Of his musical gifts she thought little. His verses
she never read. Of his romantic dreams she was
suspicious, not to say jealous. She faithfully sepa-
rated him, so far as she could, from the three things
which Martin Luther commended as the cure of
folly. He was bound, like Samson in the mill at
Gaza, to a dull, steady, interminable grind,—no
accompaniment except tinkling gossip about stupid

fashionables for whom he cared nothing,—no recreation except vapid amusements like playing Bridge with the same people night after night for money which he did not want,—no religion except attendance at St. Petronius; no intimate personal sympathy and companionship at all. He felt like a horse in a treadmill.

His only escape was in the playtime of summer and autumn when he fled to the mountains and the woods, professedly to hunt and fish, really to "loaf and invite his soul." In these outings the days of youth came back to him. Memory fingered his long-neglected violin. Imagination rebuilt those combinations of temperamental atoms on which his young fancy had climbed for a glimpse over the dividing wall between matter and spirit. What if he had followed that alluring vision and discovered that after all the ultimate atom is just a Divine idea, endowed with force by the Eternal Will?

Along with these philosophic dreams came reveries of his early friendships and comraderies in which the thoughts and desires of his heart had been intimately shared. Sometimes, in the green solitude of the forest, or floating at sundown on a lonely lake, he indulged the vagaries of that magic guide

"What If?" From these airy pathways of vision he turned smiling.

But now in these later years even those little footpaths of escape seemed to be closing. The cares of the world and the deceitfulness of riches sprang up and choked them. The fair and faithful Olivia made up her mind to be his companion everywhere, partly because she wanted to keep an eye on him, partly because her favorite doctor advised outdoor life as a preventive of fat. Even now riding across the valley he knew that his Olivia was sitting in the Chatter Box of the Double C Ranch with Mrs. Salacosa lapping up the details of the latest Philadelphia scandal. He knew also the precise words with which she would greet his return,—late as *usual!* where *have* you been? It seemed rather a dreary prospect of home-coming. But he must go ahead: there was no way out.

As he rode thus with gray care on the saddle behind him, and drew near to the foot-hills of the Giant Tetons, there came one of those theatrical effects of light for which the valley is famous. Between the clear-cut western crags a strong sunbeam slanted down upon the forest. In this illumination, as in a spotlight on the stage, a log cabin stood out from the dark woods, facing a natural meadow through which a willow-bordered brook ran with laughter. The house looked deserted for the time; a wise mongrel collie was waiting for some one in the garden-patch; a pair of vivid stellar jays bickered in the yellowing foliage of the "quakin' asps." Macrae rode up to the rail fence at the back of the yard where there was a clump of alders, and stood there, looking over.

The door of the cabin opened, and a boy of twelve or thirteen stood in the centre of the spot-light, whistling. High boots, a little run over in the heel; blue-jean overalls neatly patched on the knees; a gray flannel shirt open at the neck, round which a red kerchief was loosely knotted; an absurdly broad and floppy sombrero on the back of his head; and under the brim, black hair, a round white forehead, blue-gray eyes set wide apart, a snub nose freckled to the tip, and an Irish mouth with thin lips, now puckered in a way which made the little smiling creases at the corners disappear entirely in the enforced gravity of the whistler.

The tune was "Killarney" as John McCormack sings it, a delightfully flagrant bit of sentimentality. The boy finished it off with a flutelike trill at the end. Then the faint half-circles came back around his mouth, and he tucked his thumbs in his waistband and stepped quickly toward the small garden-patch. There was a pleasant keenness in the air that made the back of his hands and his bare neck tingle.

"Frost to-night," he said to the collie at his side, "hey, Buck? It's comin' sure. Wonder if we can fool it a little mite, old boy?"

Then he ran back to the cabin and came out in a moment with a sheet of paper, pair of scissors, and half a dozen safety-pins. The discouraged garden betrayed the havoc of the earliest touch of near winter a week ago. The sweet-potato vines trailed black along the ground; the hopeless string-beans hung limp from their poles like dead soldiers caught in an entanglement; the bright nasturtiums were all gone into a dull brown world. At the end of the patch there was a tall row of sunflowers, the boy's particular care and pride. On six of the plants a flower-head drooped dishevelled, like a yellow-haired girl with a broken neck. But on the seventh, perhaps because it had come out later and so escaped the first nip of the cold, the flower was still alive, broad-faced and beaming.

"Cheer up, old girl," said the boy, busily snipping and folding the paper, "ye've gypped one frost,—a little one,—and now I'm goin' to help ye gyp another,—a bigger one. Ground'll be all white t'morrow mornin', sure,—kind o' fairy snow,—ye can't see it fallin', and ye can't see it goin', but jes' while ye're lookin' it's gone. But it shan't git *you*, darlin'. I'll fix ye up fer the night, so's ye can see the sun fer another day, anyhow!"

So the boy talked, (like a true cow-puncher, more garrulous with dumb creatures than with people,) while his fingers fashioned the little hood that was to shelter his sweetheart overnight. Then he carefully bent the stalk of the flower toward him.

"Lean over," he said, "ye're too tall fer me. Stoop down a mite, so's I can git this on yer head. Now let me pin it here,—and here,—and here,— and here. Don't be scared. I won't stick yer neck. D'ye think I'd hurt *you?* Not fer all the world, and then some! There now,—jest a minit,—let me put in one more pin. There now, ye're all——"

"Hello there, Francie Croy," said Macrae's soft bass voice. Francie let go of the sunflower gently, and it straightened up, rustling its white hood among the leaves. Then he turned toward the high timber-fence, over which a horseman with gray hair, ruddy face, and very kind eyes, was looking at him in amusement, while his horse furtively nipped the bushes.

"Hello, Mr. Macrae," answered the boy with evident pleasure.

"What *are* you doing there?" asked Macrae. "Making bonnets for flowers? Giving first aid to the injured? Who were you talking to? I don't see anybody around."

The boy looked embarrassed, stooped to pick up the scissors and the last safety-pin which had fallen from his hand. Then he answered slowly.

"Well, ye see, it's goin' to be *some* cold, to-night. And I jes' *thought*——"

"Oh," said Macrae, "I understand. You thought you'd save the flower from freezing. Good idea. But why this particular flower? You didn't do this for the others, did you? And why were you talking to it? Flowers don't hear. What were you saying?"

Francie shook his head, looking vaguely away into the twilight, as if for words.

"I dunno," he said, "but ye see the others are all *dead*. I planted 'em all, and this is number *seven*,— lucky number! Seems like it loved the sun *most*, so

I *thought*, jes' one more *day*, p'raps two if it turns *warm*——"

"Right," said Macrae, his eyes growing kinder yet, "you are right as rain. And perhaps the flowers do hear a little, after all. Anyway, I hope so. Where's your father, boy, and your mother?"

"Dad's out, turnin' the horses on the range," answered Francie, "he'll be in soon. Mother's in the house gettin' supper. Please 'light, Mr. Macrae, and come in. I'll put your pony in the corral."

The kitchen was well warmed by the stove, on which the beans and bacon were simmering and the coffee-pot sending out whiffs of fragrant steam, while Mrs. Croy made him welcome and pulled out the most comfortable chair for him and urged him to stay to supper.

There was the faintest trace of a Killarney brogue on her tongue,—no more than a good salad recalls of the onion with which you have rubbed the inside of the bowl,—and her black hair and gray-blue eyes told her race. She must have been a very pretty colleen when her father kept the post-office in a hamlet beside Lough Leane in Queen Victoria's day. Since then she had travelled far and smiled through some rough times, as lady's maid, and children's nurse, and cook, but never lost the edge of her breeding nor the spring of her heart. When she was married, (in Boisé where she was teaching kinder-garten,) to François La Croix, ex-voyageur who had hunted and ranched his way down from Quebec through Montana and Wyoming and Utah and brought up at last in Idaho, a widower with a pair of ten-year-old sons and three thousand dollars in the bank,—when Nora Donovan married this lean, courteous, brave little man, fifteen years her senior, the ladies of the Boisé Busy Circle were inclined to endow her with their pity. But she would have none of it.

"For what," she laughed, "would those nice ladies be wasting their compassion on me? Isn't my man a fine man, and doesn't he worship the ground I tread on? He can play the fiddle better than any one of those ladies can play the melodeon. 'Tis a good name, La Croix,—Frank Croy they call him round here,—and that's a good name too, easy to speak. And for what would I be frightened of his twin boys? They're healthy young ones, and full o' fun,—'tis a good start of a family, and, glory be to God, I was never one to shun children or work. Tell those nice ladies to wait a while,—just

give me time and I'll show them who's to be
pitied!"

So the Frank Croys nested in the Teton country
and prospered in their chosen way. Time being
given, young Frank was born to a welcome, and
called Francie in his mother's tongue, to distinguish
him from his father. Old Frank was known far and
wide through the valley and beyond, as a mighty
hunter before the Lord and a wise man with cattle.
The shack grew into a ranch with a good outfit.
The twins became buckaroos of the first order and
went out cow-punching on the Buffalo Fork. Nora
kept the cabin trim and her body fit with cheerful
work; her mind free from rust by reading her ancient
favorite books and a few new magazines; and her
heart content with old Frank's love and young
Francie's growth. The boy was her harp of joy, and
his father's puzzle of pride. There was something
quaint about him. He was a good rider, afraid of
nothing, handy in the woods, already able to cook
for an outfit, and master of all his father could
teach on the fiddle. But then he often mooned,
talked to flowers and birds, hated to kill anything,
and cared less for jolly tunes than for some of those
queer things he imitated from the phonograph,—

"shirtsoes," old Frank called them. He talked to Nora about these eccentric signs.

"I 'member," he would say, "one time he shoot a beaver,—good shot, straight through head,—but Francie cry more than if he miss. Don' you think that queer? If he have,—what you call it, *du génie?* Me, I think that too. But he sure is different; not made for cowboy. I fear he shall be lonesome in Jackson Hole when we two make the round-up, old girl."

"Don't you worry about the boy," Nora would answer. "I had him under a good star. He's born to luck with enough trouble to keep him sweet. We'll stay by him as long as he needs us, and then God will see him through. Don't you believe that?"

Yes, Frank believed it, and therefore took care that the boy had enough hard work to make him tough and ready, and wondered at his fancies, and went sound asleep by the fire when he played a "shirtso" on the old violin.

Leroy Macrae knew something of this uneventful family history, and was musing over it in the kitchen while Nora set the table, and perhaps unconsciously comparing it with his own story of empty success.

The "sunflower number seven" had taken root in his mind.

In the dusk outside the cabin there was a scurry of hoofs on the gravel, a nicker of recognition as the rancher's pony joined Macrae's in the corral, a creak and a clatter as the high gate swung shut,— then Frank and the boy came in, sharp set for food. Conversation at meal-time is not the fashion in Jackson's Hole; but after supper was ended the three men went into the living-room, Frank lit the fire on the hearth, and they stretched out before it in elk-hide chairs to talk. There was an expedition planned for the next day: start at ten sharp from the Double C Ranch for a ride up Death Canyon and a couple of nights out; three pack-horses to carry the stuff; Mr. and Mrs. Macrae to ride their own ponies; Frank Croy guide, and Francie Croy cook,—that was the roster. Everything was to be ready at the dude-ranch on the river at ten o'clock to-morrow morning.

All being settled, Macrae turned to the boy.

"You like sunflowers. Do you know the story of Clytie?"

Francie nodded, for he had seen the name in his mother's "Age of Fable." Then he shook his head, for he knew by experience that his friend could make the story twice as real as any book. "You tell it," he said.

So Macrae told the tale, embroidering it as he went along. He laid the scene beside a great lake in a wild country. He made Apollo a kind of celestial sport and cattleman, immensely rich and very proud and handsome, always carrying his golden bow and arrows, for this was before guns were invented. Every day he passed above the lake from east to west in his chariot with twelve horses, driving his white cattle like clouds before him. Now Clytie was a nymph, that is to say a poor rancher's daughter, with plentiful yellow hair and large brown eyes. She fell deep in love with Apollo because he was so radiant and splendid; but he thought nothing of her, because she had only one dress of green, and that a little tattered on the edges. So he passed above her day after day without turning his head. But she looked for him in the east before the first of his horses shook its golden bit above the mountain top, and followed him with her big eyes as he rolled over the blue bridge of the sky, and looked after him long as he vanished behind the dark rim of the western forest. Nine days her fond looks thus attended her shining beloved one in his triumphal progress, and on the tenth he had compassion of her and granted her a boon. For her feet took fast hold of the earth where she was standing, and her robe was changed into broad green leaves, and she became a sunflower, with this gift, that she could turn her face as she willed from east to west, and so behold the one whom she loved from sunrise even unto sundown.

Francie nodded and smiled. He had often seen his sunflowers follow "the sunwise turn." He rose from his corner quietly, so as not to wake his father, and took the violin from its place in the cupboard. "I know the music of that story," he whispered. The piece that he played, rather slowly, was a simple version of the *intermezzo* from "Thais" as he had heard Kreisler's rendering of it on the phonograph. Old Frank slept peacefully, while Macrae thought and wondered.

Riding back to the big ranch by the river, through the moon-silvered sage-brush, past the end of Timbered Island, he could not help imagining what a difference it might make to his wife and himself if they had a boy like Francie; what a change it would work in their lives; how it might check their separating selfishness by giving them something to love and cherish together. It was a pleasant dream. But it was too late now for his wife to have a child of her own.

As he clattered down the cobbly hill of the last mesa to the open grove near the river where the orange lights of the ranch-house were glowing, he felt as if he were coming in from rather a long, happy journey. Mrs. Macrae was playing Bridge in the small office beyond the big Lazy-room where a score of young folks were stretched out on bear-skins around the open fire, softly singing. The Bridge-lady glanced up at her husband as he opened the closed door, and said, "You are late for our Bridge-party, Leroy. Where *have* you been?"

"At the Croys, making plans for our trip to-morrow. It is going to be fine."

"You took a long time making plans, it seems to me. I can't imagine what you see in those people. They say old Croy is a great bootlegger. Did you have anything to drink?"

At this there was a laugh from the three other players.

"Yes," said Macrae, rather slowly, "yes, my dear,

I had something to drink,—there was good coffee for supper and music after, and I took both."

Then he went into the Lazy-room and found a place on the floor in a corner. Soon you could hear his voice humming a bass to "The End of a Perfect Day."

II

The next morning was fair and slightly warmer, with loose clouds in the southwest. At eleven, not sharp, (Mrs. Macrae having found her stirrups, her saddle, and her mount not quite correct,) the party were ready to start. They crossed two of the broad "benches" of the mesa, and the main valley-road where a few belated Fords were still dusting and rattling toward Yellowstone Park, and took the still trail through the forest of lodge-pole pines to the Whitegrass Ranch. There they lunched with friends, and set out again about two o'clock.

To ride in that high air, seven thousand feet above the sea, was exhilarating. The forest, sombre when seen from above, was friendly green around them,— pines and spruces and Douglas firs, except in the small open glades, where golden aspens quivered and the mountain-ash berries burned red. The trail led by many a curve to the top of a granite ridge, from which they looked far down upon the lake,—lapis-lazuli set in dark malachite. Then they descended by step zigzags, cut in the face of the sheer ridge, until they reached the foaming stream which feeds the lake. By this torrent they turned, following up its course, now near, now far, on an incredibly rocky path, into Death Canyon. The precipices and crags, a thousand feet above, closed in upon them. The long ridge of Housetop and the sharp pinnacles of the Grand Teton, where the snow-fields and glaciers cling through the summer, gleamed out of the gathering clouds. In the bottom of the valley primeval tribes of the forest lingered,—huge spruces, knotted cedars, massive firs,—gigantic ancient offspring of tiny seeds. Beneath their shade the emerald mosses and yellowing ferns veiled the confusion of tumbled rocks.

When the horses stopped for a moment to take breath after a sharp scramble, Mrs. Macrae said to her husband:

"Leroy, I want to *tell* you something. I asked that man Croy just *where* we were going to make *camp* to-night, and he said he didn't *know*. Now *what* do you think of *that?*"

He explained that a really good guide hardly ever *knows* just where he is going to camp on a journey. He has some particular place in view, of course, and tries to make it at least an hour before nightfall. But the trail or the weather may be bad, the party may start late or travel slow, the light may begin to fail sooner than he expected; and then he is ready to camp in any place where he can find wood and water and a bit of level ground.

But the lady refused to be pacified by these emollient words. She was an indignant female.

"Well, *I* think it's *shameful* to send us out with a man like *that*,—not a real *guide*, only a *cowpounder*,—isn't that what you call them? I shall *complain* about him when we get back to the ranch and have him *discharged*."

Macrae said "the devil" under his breath; but the lady heard him and frowned, for she was a strict observer of all the taboos of her sect, and it was forbidden to mention the evil one except with reverence.

As the pack-train climbed slowly on, the afternoon darkened over them, the clouds folded in, the wind blew shrewdly down the gorge, and the cold rain began to spit.

"I guess we camp here," said Frank, on the edge of one of the belts of forest. The place had previously been used as a camp-ground, and had no particular beauty. But there were tent-poles and some dry wood already cut; the stream was near, and a few young balsam-firs offered their boughs for beds.

In a short time a canvas was stretched as a shelter, the provisions were unpacked, the tents pitched, a comforting fire was alight, and Francie was ready to cook the supper just as the rain settled in. But old Frank had gone up the trail to look for feed for the seven horses. He came back reporting failure.

"No good," he said, "I s'pose mus' take those horse down to head of lake. I don' like think they cold an' hungry too, all night." So he set off cheerfully on this extra journey of three miles through the wet and dark, rather than sleep while his cattle went unfed.

By the time he came back supper was over, the chilling rain mixed with hail was drumming on the canvas, and the lady, much discomforted, had crept under the tent into her sleeping-bag. A panful of corned-beef hash and a big mug of coffee were heated up for the old man, half a dozen of Francie's excellent biscuit were still warm in the baking-pot, and while old Frank addressed himself to this fare, Macrae and the boy sat on a box by the fire and talked.

Francie wanted to know about the man who had played that Clytie music for the phonograph. So Macrae told about Fritz Kreisler, what a fine fellow he was; and how he had gone to be a soldier in the war because his country called him, though she was not on the right side; and how he was wounded, and a troop of cavalry trampled over him while he was lying in a trench, and he thought he was killed, and said to himself, "God, what a stupid thing to smash a musician this way"; and how he came to his senses and felt himself, and found that only his leg was broken, and said, "God, I thank you for sparing my arms and my fingers"; and how at last he got well again, all but his game leg, and was able to play better than ever. It seemed to the boy quite a wonderful story; but he said nothing while it was told, did not even ask what country it happened in; only there was a grateful note in his voice when he said good night, and they all went to bed.

In the morning the ground was covered with

snow; the bushes were draped with heavy white cords and tassels; flurries of big white flakes whirled in the air; drifts lay in the level corners and deep crevices of the mountains; and far above, on the sharp shoulders and bold foreheads of the cliffs, the sunlight breaking through the rifted clouds made the little frosted pine-trees glitter as if they had fruited overnight in jewels. Every turn of the wind, every shift of the sky brought changes in the lighting of the titanic scene. Crags and precipices seemed to move, to draw nearer or to recede; only the high peaks, beyond the drifting cloud-rack, looked motionless. It was a miracle-morning.

But the lady was not pleased; she was too cold; the weather was abominable; it was going to snow all day; they had better go back to the ranch as soon as possible. So after old Frank had hunted up the horses, who had roamed far down the lake shore in spite of their hobbles, the packs were made, and the party set out to ride home.

This was the order of their riding: first, the guide who had not known where he was going to camp; then, the three pack-horses; then, Macrae; then his wife; and last of all, young Francie, whistling in the smooth places. The trail was wet and slippery with melting snow. It passed, at times, along the face of the steep slope, thirty or forty feet above the roaring stream. Mrs. Macrae had been advised, the day before, not to ride in what seemed to her the safest place, the extreme inside of the path, lest her horse, striking against some jutting rock or boulder, might be startled or thrown over the outer edge and so down the gorge. But she rather prided herself on the skill she had attained as a horse-woman in the park; moreover, this morning she was particularly nervous and high-strung, so she rode her own way, with a tight, worrying rein, and as close as she could get to the rocks.

The probable happened. Her puzzled and irritated pony bumped against a projecting corner, was shoved out, made a few excited false steps, and slithered over the edge. Macrae with difficulty turned his pony and clattered back, grasping at her bridle. But the boy was quicker, and rode along a little ledge below her to block her fall if possible. It was too late. Her horse struck his too heavily; both fell; it was a bad mix-up. The lady was luckily tossed into a clump of stiff bushes and escaped with a great scare and a few scratches. The boy clung to his mount longer, went farther down the slope, was rolled upon, and lay among the rocks with his leg broken.

In justice to Mrs. Macrae it must be told that she behaved well in the serious emergency. She forgot her own bruises and helped her husband make the boy as comfortable as possible, while his father rode down to the lower end of the lake for help. Francie did not talk much, but once he said something to her husband that she did not understand.

"Jes' like the fellow who played that Clytie music, ain't it?"

Macrae nodded.

"Yes," he said in rather a shaky voice, "it is like him. He came out all right, and made a lot more music, and so will you, Francie."

They had a hard time getting him down to the J. Y. Ranch on the lake. From there they rushed him in an automobile over to the neat little hospital at Jackson. The Macraes settled down in the hotel and Nora Croy came in from the foot-hills as fast as a horse could bring her. There was no lack of nurses for the wounded soldier.

The doctor's prognosis was favorable. The boy was not dangerously injured, there was no internal damage, he was almost certain to get well, and quickly. But the broken leg was rather a bad one. Here the doctor went into a learned explanation about thigh-bones and fractures and ball-and-socket joints. "The boy will be all right," he concluded, "but he is pretty sure to have a game leg as long as he lives. Perhaps he can ride a soft pony, but not well,—he will never make a first-class buckaroo."

Macrae smiled.

"Sorry he has to give that up, doctor," said he. "It's a fine life. But there are others."

It was a few days after this conversation that Macrae told his wife about it and some other things.

"And so you see," he went on, "the Croys have agreed that as soon as Francie is well enough, he is coming east to live with us, to go to school, and especially to study music, for I think he has the hand and the spirit of a fine violinist, perhaps another Albert Spalding."

"But Leroy," she said, "you ought to have asked me sooner."

"My dear," he replied, with a look in his eyes which he did not often show to her, "I am not *asking* you now; I am just *telling* you. This is the plan we have made. There are only two people who could possibly spoil it,—you or the boy. I believe

you are both going to love it and make it a success."

She took it wonderfully well. In her heart she
had already begun to care for the boy, knowing that
he had saved her from disfigurement, possibly from
death, and feeling in him something rare and precious
that could add a new and distinguished interest to
her life,—a famous violinist,—that would be splendid!

The same evening Macrae sat by the boy's bed
with his mother, and told him of the plan. His eyes
shone, and he looked a question to his mother. She
nodded her head, and smiled bravely.

"The school is a very nice one," Macrae went on,
"and there will be plenty of fellows to play with.
And you are to have my old violin, a beauty, smooth
as silk, brown as a beaver, sings like a bird. It can
talk too: you can make it say anything you like, the
Clytie story or anything else."

Francie was silent for a minute, looking out of
the window. Then he spoke.

"You 'member that sunflower number seven?
Mother put the hood on her all right the night we
were up at Death Canyon. But the hard frost was
too much for her. She died. I'm very sorry. But

I think she brought me luck. That violin'll be fine, and I'll like to live with you, Mr. Macrae, and learn music."

This was a long speech for Francie. When he ended, the little smiling half-circles came back around the corners of his mouth. Nora Croy smiled too, while she wiped her eyes. And Macrae looked like a man in the woods who has found a lost trail.

A GARDEN ENCLOSED

A GARDEN ENCLOSED

WHEN Judge Effingham built the high wall around his spacious garden at Calvinton there was much discussion among the neighbors about the meaning of this innovation. Everything new or unusual in that quiet and mildly inquisitive burgh caused talk and speculation as to its purpose. People were always curious, but generally too dignified to ask what a thing was for. They preferred to guess, and then draw conclusions from the motive which they assigned to the novelty. The majority were inclined to look for a good reason. But there was a little coterie that liked better to find or invent a bad one. Even among the Olympians, you know, there were some jealous and suspicious divinities.

"That wall is an exhibition of selfishness," said one. "The judge put it up so that he could have his flowers all to himself. He doesn't want anybody else to enjoy them."

"It looks to me more like pride and ambition," said another. "He likes to have something different and superior about his place. That wall is rather ostentatious, don't you think? He was on the Superior Court in Pennsylvania, you know, and I suppose he can't come down from his high perch, though he has retired from office."

But these foolish guesses about the wall were put out of countenance when that very bold and lively old lady, Mrs. Black, went to the judge and asked him pointblank:

"Why did you build that wall?"

"Madam," he answered with the courteous and somewhat elaborate manner which he used to all ladies, "I erected the enclosure, which to my great regret does not seem to excite your admiration, for purely horticultural reasons, in order to create an asylum or sanctuary for my flowers and shrubs. The wind,—but first will you allow me to give you a brief exposition of my theory of life?"

"Hmph," said Mrs. Black, "not necessary, but go ahead if you want to."

"Well," he continued, "I am what may be called a Christian dualist. I hold that those ideas which were expressed by the great Persian philosopher Zarathustra are still valid. The world is the arena of a perpetual conflict between good and evil, light and darkness, life and death, expressed in various forces and principles, which oppose each other and contend together constantly. Now the wind, which in some respects, if not abnormally violent, is beneficial to the tall and sturdy trees because it seems to exercise and develop their strength in resisting it,—the wind is the enemy of the lowly and lovely flowers. They can only develop their full life and beauty when some kind of a protective shelter is provided for them. It is therefore the duty of a Christian dualist who is also an intelligent horticulturist to defeat the inimical wind by enclosing——"

"Quite so!" interrupted the lively old lady. "I get your point. I'll put a stop to this silly gossip about the wall. But how shall we see your garden to know whether you are right?"

"By visiting it, madam," he answered with an old-fashioned bow. "The more frequently you and our neighbors come to enjoy my flowers the more pleased and honored I shall be."

It was in truth a delicious retreat, that garden planted westward in Calvinton on the soft rondure of the hill that sloped gently down to the green vale of Sunny Stream and the larger wooded valley of Stony Brook.

The old burgh itself was not exactly a noisy place,

except along the highway where the gigantic motor-trucks rumbled with their heavy loads and the swift pleasure-cars snorted and panted with their mufflers wide open for speed's sake. Otherwise it was a tranquil town. There was rarely a racket, save when an intercollegiate football-game was on, or when the students varied their ardent intellectual pursuits with a loud "pee-rade." To come back from roaring New York, or even from rattling Philadelphia, to the classic shades of Calvinton was like a return from Babel to Eden.

But within that general calm there was a centre of deeper repose; within those sanctuary precincts a shrine of peace. It was Effingham's garden enclosed. There the high-vaulted elms, round-headed maples, and wide-armed apple-trees, relics of an ancient orchard, cast their moon-spun or sun-woven shadows on smooth verdant lawns. There little pathways meandered among thickets of flowering shrubbery, where rhododendrons glistened and glowed, pink dogwoods blushed divinely, and Persian lilacs shed their delicate fragrance on the air. There climbing roses covered the tall conical arbors built of cedar poles, like Indian teepees, with rich roofing of red, or yellow, or snow-white. There, in the beds and borders, the earliest flowers of spring rose miraculously from their earthy graves,—pale snowdrop, golden crocus, sapphire scilla, purple hyacinth; and after that a flood-tide of rainbow-tinted tulips; and after that the gorgeous peonies and the stately irises; and after that the clustered bells of lilies, and the summer-swords of gladiolus, and the swaying stars of cosmos, the flames of scarlet sage, and the autumnal tints of perennial chrysanthemums. Each season of time, in smooth relative succession, brought its own tribute of blossom to attest, with florid signature, the reality of the flowing months, and to prove that in this dual world where Ormuzd and Ahriman are at strife, the flowers are grateful for protection from their enemy the wind.

But the finest bloom of the little paradise was Lillace Effingham,—sole daughter of her father's house and heart. There was something cloistral in her beauty, though it was in no way frail or morbid. The rose of health was on her cheeks, her gray eyes were lit with intelligence and wonder—the eyes of a child who sees something new in every day. Yet she seemed always a creature set apart from the rude contacts of the world, as if her innocent serenity lay deep within her like a crystal pool which no rough wind had ever moiled or darkened. Her thoughts and visions walked in white. Not dull nor ignorant; quick-minded, joyful-hearted; she was a little sister of happiness, a nun of pure delight.

In effect she was just the reverse of the girl in Hawthorne's strange story of "Rappaccini's Daughter." All the pains which the weird Italian had taken to imbue his Beatrice with the deadly breath and sap of poisonous flowers, Effingham had spent upon his Lillace to make her like a cup full of vital joy, a plant whose flowers and leaves were rich in healing. She had tutors; she went to school for a couple of years; but the guidance of her education was in her father's hands, and he loved it.

There was nothing narrow and censorious about that education: no bans and barriers: no taboos of superstition.

"Read what you like," he said to her; "but make sure to find out why you like it. And if the reason leaves a bad taste in your mouth, give it up."

He taught her to read and write French admirably. Her favorite authors were Lamartine, Victor Hugo, Sully-Prudhomme, and Maurice de Guérin,—rare tastes for a young woman, but to her as natural as the air she breathed. In "The Crime of Sylvestre

Bonnard," Anatole France charmed her; but in his later work, though the limpid style was still enchanting, there was something repellent, mordant, satanic.

"It is a wonderful paradise of words," she said, "but there are too many serpents in it. And the apples have rotten spots. It wouldn't be pleasant to get a liking for rotten spots."

Her father taught her a little Persian also, just enough to illustrate his favorite judgment that Firdausi was far superior, as a poet, to the much-quoted Omar Khayyam.

"Fitzgerald's translation made Omar's reputation," said the judge. "The Persians rank him as a good astronomer but a second-rate poet."

Lillace accepted the critical judgment in deference to her father's general (but sometimes annoying) habit of being right. But her romantic fancy still cherished some of the sad quatrains of the "Rubaiyat."

On the whole, the life of the garden enclosed was happy and not without temperate rejoicing. Passionate storms did not enter there. Even the Great War did not shatter its tranquillity. The old judge played his part as a patriot by subscribing to Liberty Loans and publicly denouncing William Hohenzollern as an incarnation of Ahriman, the God of Evil. Mrs. Effingham,—a lady as delicate and beautiful as a bit of antique point-lace,—busied her white hands indefatigably with knitting socks and sweaters for the soldiers, while her thoughts travelled

"The marvellous current of forgotten things."

Lillace was keen to go abroad as a nurse, but her father would not hear of it. So she threw herself eagerly into all the eddies of war-work that swirled through Calvinton,—Red Cross auxiliaries, Navy League chapters, Army Aid groups, societies for rolling bandages and packing ditty-bags, teas for the A. O. T. C. in the college, and dances for the U. S. N. R. F. in the graduate school. From these activities she came back to the quiet garden refreshed as an Oread from a bath in the sea.

Then came the armistice,—the day of jubilation; the sudden, stunning dead-stop of war; the slow, dallying, confused, baffling, foiling return of peace. It was in these months of hope deferred that Mrs. Effingham drifted gently out of life,—a bit of rare old lace worn very thin and carried away by an unseen breeze. The flowers of the garden enclosed were spread over her grave. A year later the judge went out on the long last voyage of discovery to test the truth of that Christian dualism which he had held so sturdily.

So Lillace was left alone. To tend her garden; to rule her house, full of books and pictures and ancient treasures; to enjoy the "modest competency," (as we used to call it,) of the estate which was left to her; to continue the placid friendships of her earlier years; and to complete the fine translation of the "*Librès Méditations*" of Sénancour which she had begun before the war: these were the things she had to do, and she did them very happily.

It was not long after the publication of her exquisite book,—so pellucid, so pure, so tremulous with the potency of deep natural feeling,—that the event happened which brought peril to the garden enclosed.

I know not how to describe her psychic state at this time so that the reader shall see it as clearly as I felt it, and feel it still. She was contented, yet not satisfied; she had rest, but not repose; her dreams were perfect save in the touch of reality; she was ready to believe all that attracted her, yet timorous to adventure the loss of her long-cherished peace. Her spring was past; her summer waned; her autumn delayed; winter was a distant threat.

Perhaps a passage from Sénancour will be more revealing than my clumsy attempts at description. This is what he says:

"When an irresistible feeling carries us far beyond the things that are ours, and fills us first with rapture, then with regret, giving us a vision of blessings which are out of our reach, this deep and fleeting sense is but the inner proof of the superiority of our faculties over our destiny. And for this reason it lingers but for a while, and is soon changed to regret; it is enchanting, then heartrending, . . . We suffer for not being what we might be; but were we to find ourselves in that order of things for which we long, we should no longer have either that excess of desire or that redundance of faculties; we should no longer enjoy the delight of being above our destiny, greater than our environment, more productive than we have need to be. . . . The things of actual life would no longer be of service to bear us beyond, into the imaginary region of the ideal brought into subjection to the sovereignty of actual man. But why should these things be purely ideal? That is what I cannot understand."

Such was the attitude of Lillace Effingham's mind and heart in her twenty-ninth year, when she met

Captain Basil Fitz Roy at a state dinner in Harmon House. His presence was accounted for as a retired British Army officer, invalided out of service by reason of serious injuries received in the war,—wounded twice and severely gassed,—in fact very badly knocked about and used up. He was now travelling to regain his health and employing the opportunity to study American methods of military education. This had brought him on a visit to Calvinton, where there was a mathematical gunnery school attached to the college. Some one had put him up at the Town and Gown Club and he was received as a distinguished foreigner in the best social ellipses of the burgh.

"Very smart," said old Mrs. Black. "Talks just like a new English novel. Notice how he clips the 'g' off the ends of his words? Wonder where he comes from besides the army. They say he gets no English mail at the club,—except things that look like bills."

But beyond a doubt Captain Fitz Roy was the most noticeable male person at the dinner where he met Miss Effingham. He belonged to the lean type of Englishman, tall, well set up, fairly heavy in the shoulders, and distinctly thin in the waist. His hair

was black and smooth; his dark hazel eyes were large
and deep-set under arched brows; his face was pale,
though you could see it had once been well bronzed,
and there were many lines upon it, notably two deep
creases around the corners of his nose, and a long
white scar on his left temple close to the hair. He
looked about thirty-five years old, but it was impossible to tell his age. He might have been just under
thirty or just over forty. He was evidently a man
with a past—presumably heroic, certainly adventurous. He talked well, but not much about himself,
and not at all about the war. On that subject he refused to be drawn. But he seemed to know most of
the people worth knowing in England and France,
and to have a store of illuminating remarks to make
about them.

Lillace, whom he took in to dinner, was fascinated
by him from the first. She listened to him intently
and found something charmingly frank and simple
in his very reserves.

"Lloyd George?" he said in answer to her question, "yes, I know him, but not well. I doubt if any
one does. He has very little private life, you know;
it's almost all for the platform. He's what you call
in this country a 'spellbinder,' if you understand

what I mean. He stands up and smiles at the audience and they all adore him. Then he gets confidential and tells them a lot of things they know already, and they think it's wonderful. Then he winds up with a burst of eloquence and a snappy phrase, and the house rises at him and lifts the roof with applause."

Lillace felt as if she had been at the meeting. She went on to ask about other French and English personages. Of all the captain had something interesting to tell.

"Anatole France," he said, "is a most extraordinary old chap. I breakfasted with him twice,—in Tours and in Paris. You know his real name is Jacques Thibault, but they all call him Anatole,—or *cher maître* when they want to be polite. He lives in the most extraordinary way. Something like a mixture of Voltaire and one of the old Hebrew patriarchs surrounded by,—er,—ladies. With words he's a genius, but in other matters his taste is atrocious."

So their talk rambled on over persons and books and things till it seemed to Lillace as if she were on a thrilling excursion far away from the familiar precincts of the old burgh and its well-groomed gardens.

Of course the inevitable question had to be asked: "How do you like America?"

"I don't *like* it," answered Fitz Roy with his big sombre eyes lighting up as he looked into hers. "I *love* it. May I come to see you one day and tell you how much and why? Then perhaps I can talk to you a little about the war, if you wish it, but not here, to all these people."

She admitted shyly that she wished it. He came to call not only one day but many days. In fact he became an almost daily visitor, besides showing her marked deference and attention when they met in other places. They had afternoon tea on the veranda; little dinners with two or three other guests, or *tête-à-tête*. In the mellow light of the Hunter's Moon they walked the paths of the garden enclosed or sat together on a wooden bench under a spreading apple-tree. Evidently it was an "affair," and Calvinton soon began to gossip about it.

"Very romantic," said some. "A real case of love at first sight." (The members of the *Alliance Fran-çaise* preferred to call it *coup de foudre*, which sounded more knowing.) "But wasn't it lucky for Lillace, after waiting so long, to have such an intriguing man come after her?"

"Hmph," said Mrs. Black, who had begun to have serious doubts about the gallant captain. "*Intriguing* is a new-fangled word, but I guess it's right. Instead of love at first sight, this may be a case of fortune-hunting at close range. Who knows anything about this Fitz Roy? I've inquired at the British Embassy in Washington and written to my old friend General Desmond in London, but can't get a word. There's a wall around that garden, but there ought to be a caretaker for that girl."

The general popularity of the captain had declined considerably. His manners were beautifully British, but his habits were a bit queer. He never came down to breakfast, but began the day with a meal which he called "brunch." Sometimes he was very jolly in a restrained way, bright as a new half-crown, and other times he was dull and heavy, plainly depressed and nervous, almost gloomy. These alternations he explained briefly as the result of a malarial fever caught in the marshes around Salonika. But some of the men thought they were the effects of a secret devotion to that adamantine liquor which came into the United States with the Volstead law, or perhaps of a too fond affection for the hypodermic needle. There was nothing certain against him, but the fellows who had trained in England and served in France thought it rather strange that they had never seen Fitz Roy, nor even heard of him, until they met him in Calvinton as the open admirer of Lillace Effingham.

To her none of these suspicions came. She was not the kind of a girl to whom people repeat scandal. In her presence, to her eyes, the captain was all that a hero of romance should be; eager, respectful, serious with a touch of wit, a most persuasive talker.

He was in effect a hunter by race and by experience, a very Nimrod of feminine hearts. He knew the difference between the two kinds of girls: those who may be won by a bold assault, conquering the way to the soul through the senses; and those with whom discretion is the better part of valor and whose entire surrender depends upon the winning of their inmost thoughts and feelings first. The wise hunter knew that his present game was of this latter type. So he went cautiously about the chase.

His three effective weapons were his eloquent enthusiasm for her ideals; his grave, ardent praise of her beauty; and his vivid recital of his own adventures and exploits. The becoming reticence on this last point which marked his general conversation quite disappeared when he was talking to her alone. It was a courtship somewhat in the Victorian manner, but still more in the older manner of Othello. He had the air of not wishing to boast of his heroic deeds, but he told about them at full length.

"It was nothing," he would say. "All the other chaps would have done the same, or better, if the chance had come to them."

"But tell me about it," she urged, "I never heard anything so splendid. Tell me how you felt when you came up against the German machine-gun hidden in the wood where you were scouting with only two men. Tell me what you did to that Prussian captain when he slashed your head with his sword after he had surrendered. Is that the scar on your temple? Tell me all about it."

So the captain, with assumed reluctance, went on to speak

"of most disastrous chances,
Of moving accidents by flood and field,
Of hairbreadth 'scapes i' the imminent deadly breach,"

while his gentle Desdemona "seriously inclined to hear" his tales, and the more she heard the more she admired and adored this figure of a noble, valiant man of action.

He understood very well that she knew little or nothing about the history and actual events of the war, and this gave him all the freer hand in weaving his vivid tapestry of things he had read and remembered. He could put himself on two distant fronts at the same time. He could be in the cavalry, the artillery, and aviation. He could do the incredible, if not the impossible.

In April 1915 he was in the trenches of Ypres when that horrible green cloud of poison-gas rolled down upon the dismayed Allies. The same month he was landing on a blood-stained beach at Gallipoli, fighting his way desperately through barbed wire and a tempest of machine-gun fire to a position on top of the barren, rocky cliff. He was with Townshend in the hell-fire of Mesopotamia and with Haig in the frozen inferno of Loos. He was all over the map. Everywhere he praised his men, their pluck and patience and bulldog grip. But his Desdemona was always thinking:

"If *they* were brave, how much braver must their *captain* have been? The man who led them, this man who is now talking to me!"

With his discourse of battles he mingled praise of peace as the normal state of man.

"War is a horror," he said, "a wide-awake nightmare, a cruel, crazy thing. Wasn't it your old General Sherman who said 'war is hell'? When a chap comes to it he has to wade through it for his country's sake, of course. But when he comes out he ought to pray and work to make its return impossible. That's what the League of Nations is for. That's what the British and American fleets are for. That's what the Anglo-Saxon race wants and will always be ready to fight for,—Peace!"

These sentiments in a soldier seemed to Lillace thrillingly fine. But even more thrilling were the personal sentiments toward herself which he allowed himself to express with discreet fervor. He was careful not to alarm her modesty by touch or gesture. He knew that his bird was timid and must be approached gently. But his words were ardent.

"Even when he is fighting," said he, "or slogging at a long march, or shivering in the trenches, a man has his ideal, his beautiful dream to console him. You were my dream. I couldn't see your face, didn't know your name. But now I see you and know you, and my dream comes true. Lillace, I love you more than tongue can tell."

He took her hand and raised it to his lips. The moonlight in the garden fell full upon her face. He saw it blanch and her lips tremble. His bird was frightened. He must not go too fast, must not "rush his fences." He laid her hand back upon her knee, as if it were something sacred. Her eyes were turned to him very seriously. Then she looked down.

"I like you," she murmured, "more than any man I have ever met. But I know you so little. It all seems so strange to me."

"I will tell you everything about myself," he said, "you shall know everything there is to know. I was well off once, but I'm pretty poor now. However, I'm able to work again, and I have good prospects and plenty of strong friends. I was married when I was only a boy. My wife was not of my class. She was careless and extravagant, but she was a good girl, and pretty, and loyal. I was devoted to her. She died the second year I was in France. Our only child died six months before her. It nearly broke my heart. See, here is her picture."

He pulled from his pocketbook a faded photograph of the type that used to be called *carte-de-visite*. She looked at it with swimming eyes. How strange it was for him to show her this now! There was something,

"The new day has come for me.   The future is with you."

too, in the words he had spoken which vaguely troubled her.

The picture showed a woman of about twenty-five, pretty in a commonplace way, with curiously arched eyebrows and an appealing, puzzled look in her eyes like that of a faithful dog. She was dressed in plain black.

"That was taken soon after our child died," said Fitz Roy. "She sent it to me in France. I always carry it with me. But it all belongs to the past now. Please keep the picture. The new day has come for me. The future is with you. My own lovely dream come true, I adore you. Will you marry me?"

He moved toward her, but was stayed by her look, her unconscious gesture.

"You must give me time," she said. "This is very serious. I must think it over alone. Will you come back to-morrow afternoon at five? No one else will be here. Good night."

She put out her hand to him. It trembled a little in his. He almost thought it returned his grasp as he bent over it. The silvery chime of Trinity Church was striking half after nine when he passed out of the garden. Lillace went into the house for a shawl and came back to another bench to sit in the moonlight, looking now at the faded picture, now at the pale cosmos flowers against the wall.

The steps on the grass behind her were so light that she did not hear them, but she felt that some one was near her. She looked up and saw a woman dressed in black, with curiously arched eyebrows and an appealing look in her eyes, staring out of a face once pretty but now worn and pathetic. At first she thought it must be a ghost,—the ghost of the dead woman whose picture lay on her lap.

"I beg your pardon," said the woman in a low, pleasant voice, "but are you Miss Effingham?"

"That is my name," answered Lillace, controlling herself with an effort, "but how did you find your way here, and why have you come so late?"

"I hope I am not too late," replied the visitor, "I hope to God I am not too late! They told me at the Inn that you lived here, in the house with a wall around the garden. They told me, too, that my husband is in this town and that he comes to see you every day. Is that true?"

Lillace looked at the photograph and back again at the face of the woman. The likeness was unmistakable.

"Do you mean Captain Basil Fitz Roy?"

"That's what he calls himself now, I believe. He has a dozen names, but his real one is Ben Fitts,— the same initials, you see, that I marked on his linen. That is my picture on your lap. Don't you recognize it? Do you want me to tell you about him?"

It was a terrible moment. The garden enclosed seemed to be rocking and whirling about its mistress. The protecting wall was down and a death-cold wind from the north crept over it. She had no shelter now except her simple faith and her virgin honor.

"Yes," she said. "I want you to tell me about him. Sit down here beside me, please, and tell me quietly all the truth and nothing else."

"I thank you for your kindness," said the woman, sobbing a little. "I was afraid you would despise me. But now I know you are good. It is not an easy story to tell. Ben and I were married eight years ago, while he was in the service. He was a higher class than me, better educated and always very clever. I had a bit of money, not much, but enough to make things easier for him. I believe he was real fond of me then. He was never a captain, you know; just a clerk in the commissariat, but always a beautiful talker, never in the fighting. Then something went wrong with his accounts. I'll never believe he stole, but they said he did, so he had to slip away and hide. I helped him. They didn't look for him too hard, because he had some strong friends who wanted him to get off. It was then he took up changing his name. With his cleverness and my bit of money we got along well enough. We had three children. One died. The others are with my sister in England now."

She paused for a minute in her steady narrative while she wiped her eyes, and sobbed. Silent tears were running down the cheeks of Lillace. Her heart was compressed and twisted in her side as if a hard hand had grasped it and were trying to tear it out by the roots. But she made no movement, no outcry. Her sudden sorrow and shame lay upon her heavy as frost and deep as death.

If this strange visitor were real,—a living woman of flesh and blood, and of that Lillace had a fatal certainty,—then her own dawning love for Fitz Roy was a false dawn, a cruel delusion, a thing to make her tingle with reproach and humiliation. The bright image of a hero of romance that she had created in her garden enclosed, changed dreadfully before her eyes. It was clothed in ragged ignominy and foul deceit. It mocked her trustfulness with grinning lips and outthrust tongue. It leered at her with angry eyes of greed and disappointment. She could almost hear it jeering,—"I nearly had you in my arms,— you were willing,—by a hair's breadth only I missed you, my little lady!"

How was this to be met? By the primitive woman, no doubt, with fierce anger, hot resentment, and revenge if possible. But what good would these do to the heart of Lillace? They were weapons that she could not use without a deeper shame. After all, the wrong done her was nothing compared with the wrong done to this sobbing woman at her side. A saying from an old book that she loved to read glowed in her mind: *If troubles overwhelm thee, find deliverance in a good deed.* On that she steadied, and turned to her visitor with a great kindness in her look.

"I believe all that you have told me," she said. "Now, if you are a little rested, and can do it without distress, won't you go on and tell me more about your life?"

"I'll say we were happy enough till Ben took to drinking and using drugs. Then we had some hard, rough times, and had to live in some mean dirty places. When he was himself he was the perfect gentleman, lovely to look at and listen to. But when he was full it seemed like a devil entered into him. You noticed that white scar on his forehead. He got that in a fight in a bar. You see this crooked elbow on me? (She pulled up her sleeve.) That's where my arm broke one night when he threw me downstairs. Then my money ran very low. Ben started out on his travels, looking for a job, he said. But I never knew what he was doing. Once in a while he'd send me a little money, but he never gave me his real address. It was always some post-office. I got work in a milliner's shop, and was living with my sister who runs a fancy laundry in the West End, but it was awful lonely, spite of the children. He was in Buenos Aires for a while; then he came to the States to do some university work, he said. I just couldn't live without him any longer. So I parked the children with sister and came over to look for him and got on his track and found that he was here. Everybody said he was making love to you. But I'm his wife. Look, here are my marriage lines. I love him still, spite of everything. Dear lady, won't you give him back to me?"

"No, my friend," said Lillace, whose eyes were now cleared of weeping, "I won't give him back because he is not mine. He is yours. I'll send a note to him, and he shall come for you in the morning to take you home. I'll finance the journey. You are going to sleep in my guest-room to-night. Come, no excuses. You got here just at the right time, and I'm very grateful to you. Now let's go to bed. We are both very tired."

What was in Lillace Effingham's note no one except Ben Fitts ever knew. But he came early in the morning and took his wife away with him. The garden is still enclosed and May is filling it with radiant virginal bloom.

A BLIND LAMPLIGHTER

A BLIND LAMPLIGHTER

"**I** USED to see him going his rounds in B——," said my old schoolmate Charles Frost, (whom nobody could call a sentimentalist, for he was inclined by nature to be rather hard and a doubter,) "in those days after we graduated from the 'Poly' I often saw David Gray tapping his way along the streets, busy with his odd task of lamp-lighting. It always gave me a curious feeling. There was something incongruous about it. Singular, that a man just so handicapped should have just that work to do, and that he should do it so well, seem to find so much satisfaction in it. It puzzled me; and you know I like to understand and explain everything if possible.

"How long ago this was you may judge from the fact that the lamps which he lighted were gas-burners. You remember them? They were enclosed in square glass lanterns, perched on iron posts eight or ten feet high,—just about the right height to tempt mischievous boys to throw stones at them when the 'cop' was not in sight. The lamp-posts stood at the street-corners, and sometimes there was one in the middle of a long block. The light which they shed was not dazzling,—a faint, fulvous illumination at best; and when the burner was half stoppered by rust or by an accumulation of gritty dust, it gave out only a broken yellow fan of pale radiance, pierced by a blue streak of shrill whistling flame.

"But after all the street-lamps were an immense improvement on the primitive oil-lanterns which made darkness visible when B—— was a growing village. They served to embarrass nervous robbers, to cheer the yawning policeman on his beat, to guide the belated citizen on his homeward way. The iron posts were a godsend to the fuddled reveller who embraced them and clung to them while he regained his lost balance and courage to pursue his zigzag journey.

"Old David Gray took a lot of pride in his job. I don't know why I should call him 'old,' except that we often use that word for a man that we really like, —you know how the French say 'mon vieux,'—and the English 'old thing.' But Gray was about thirty when I first met him as a lamplighter. It turned out that I had known him before.

"It was just before sunset on one of those cool, clear, October evenings when the saffron glow is held long in the western sky, exquisite, regretful. Something in his face was familiar. I watched him at his work. He did it deftly.

"In his right hand he carried a stick about six feet long. At the upper end it had a metal contrivance for opening the doors of the glass lanterns and turning the cocks of the burners, and some kind of a lamp covered with a tin cylinder for lighting the gas. The whole thing was done with three motions in half a minute. The lower end of the stick he used as a cane, tapping the pavement before him now and then, but not all the time. He seemed to know his way about almost as if he were walking in his own room. You would hardly have thought him blind but for the thick blue spectacles that completely covered his eyes. A seeing man would not have worn these at twilight.

"As I looked at him more closely the familiarity of his face came out more clearly. He was undoubtedly a former clerk in my father's shipping-office. As a boy I had known him well and liked him a lot. He was a quiet, plodding fellow, always cheerful, and very friendly in supplying me with those 'shipping-cards' which we boys used to collect. You remember them,—'The White Dove,' 'The Swift Arrow,' 'Fly-

ing Eagle,' 'Queen of the Sea,' 'Sailor's Darling.'
The cards, in addition to mercantile information,
displayed wonderful mid-Victorian pictures. The
good-natured fellow had helped me to make a larger
collection of these art treasures than any of the other
boys. Of course I was grateful in a boy's dumb and
awkward way. And now——

"'Is that you, Mr. Gray?' I asked.

"'Yes, Mr. Charles, this is David Gray,' he answered, recognizing my way of speaking instantly.

"Then I started to say a fool thing. 'Shake hands.
You've had an ac—,' but some instinct stopped me,
and I went on a better tack. 'You've got a new job,
I see.'

"'Yes, and a good one too,—lighting up things.
Your father got it for me. But please excuse me, I
must hurry on now,—thirty more lamps to tend before dark.'

"I asked him if I might walk with him, and he
readily agreed. As we paced those quiet streets he
outlined his story very modestly. When the Civil
War broke out he wanted to enlist, but my father
dissuaded him. He had a young wife and a baby.
Then came the draft. But his name was not drawn.

"A rich abolitionist, who was very fierce about

'smashing the South' but had no stomach for facing personal danger, offered a thousand dollars for a substitute to go to the war in his place. Gray did not care a hoot from Hades about abolitionism, nor about the millionaire. He couldn't see why the United States didn't pay the slave-owners and emancipate the slaves, as England had done,—that would have cost far less than a war. But he was ready,—yes, keen,—to fight for the saving of the Union and the honor of his country. Moreover, the bonus money would be extremely useful to his little family.

"So he accepted it and went to the war. One of war's terrible things promptly happened to him. A lighted grenade had fallen beside an ammunition dump, and lay there sizzling. It threatened death to a hundred men. Gray ran and picked it up to throw it into the river. The brute thing exploded as it left his hand and put out both of his eyes forever.

"He was well nursed in hospital, well cared for in the blind asylum, taught to read with his fingers, to weave baskets and rugs, and all that sort of thing. But that would not support his wife and child. What could he do?

"He did not have the peculiar gift that a good piano-tuner needs, but it seems that he had a quite remarkable instinct for finding his way in the dark which perpetually surrounded him. Lead him over a path once and he could follow it again inerrantly. It was like a seventh sense. He felt the points of the compass in his mind. He had 'an ear practised like a blind man's touch.' He had also that patient cheerfulness, that touching alertness, which so often beautifies those who cannot see with their eyes.

"There was a place open for a lamplighter in B——. My father recommended him for it, and backed him warmly. After some hesitation it was agreed to take him on trial. At first his wife went with him on his rounds. But he soon passed beyond the need of her aid. He knew his way all right; he was regular, dependable, 'calm as a clock,' as they say in Maine. I recall his saying on one of our earlier walks, 'Nowadays my little girl sometimes comes with me. But it isn't for guidance, it's just for company. Here is my last lamp. To-morrow I must come around at daybreak to put them all out. But you know, Mr. Charles, dusk and dawn make no difference to me.'

"So we shook hands good-night. Many a time have I walked a mile or two with him since then. I used to visit him occasionally in his home,—three small rooms on a narrow street, but his wife kept them wonderfully bright and clean.

"He regretted that the 'movies' were no good to him, but thought that his small phonograph was a God-given compensation. He had a set of records of religious music, hymns and anthems, sung by a fine church choir. He used to turn them on, Sunday mornings, and hum a doubtful bass accompaniment. But Sunday nights he preferred to go with his wife to some plain meeting-house where the singing was hearty and he could 'join in.' He knew the old hymns by heart. His favorite was:

> 'Sun of my soul, thou Saviour dear,
> It is not night if Thou art near.'

"When the gas-lamps were replaced by electricity he was retired on a small pension. If he could have lived to hear the radio, he would have regarded it as a special miracle wrought for the blind and the hard of hearing. He liked to philosophize half humorously about the strange contrast between his condition and his work,—giving people light which he could not see. He had a singular pleasure in recalling it. He often said: 'There are many things in life which we can help others to enjoy though we can't get them for ourselves.'

"Good thought to steer by, that. If it's true, Gray sees why it's true, now.

"You know, my friend," continued Frost, "I am what they call an agnostic. I cannot feel as sure of God and the soul as you seem to do. But I am sure there was something in that blind lamplighter which scientific chemistry and biology cannot explain, something which darkness can never conquer. When one of my heavy despondent moods comes over me,— and every honest agnostic has them,—I think of David Gray and remember Wordsworth's lines in 'Resolution and Independence,'—

'I could have laughed myself to scorn to find
In that decrepit man so firm a mind.'"

A GARMENT OF PRAISE

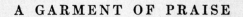

A GARMENT OF PRAISE

During a year of active service in the American Navy, with a roving commission for all the naval stations, I learned far more than I taught. Many genial officers and their wives hospitably entertained the itinerant chaplain and refreshed him with curious stories of life, love, and adventure on the "West African Station" and other romantic homes of myth and legend. The following tale is really too short and slight to be called a story—it is only a sketch.

It was given to me by the veteran Rear-Admiral B——, while we sat smoking one night on the broad veranda of the Commandant's House in the ancient navy-yard of Portsmouth, beneath the spreading silver maples and trembling aspens, where Roosevelt had led the feet of the Russian and Japanese envoys toward the path of peace in 1905, and where the hum and hammering of equipment for the World War were faintly heard under the August moon of 1918. At that time, in those surroundings, with the admiral's gentle Southern wife knitting beside us in a mercifully silent rocking-chair, his very simple narrative seemed to have a certain significance which went deep into the springs of human conduct. Perhaps it threw a little light on one of the hidden causes of the personal misunderstandings and domestic strifes and international wars which vex and hamper this poor mortal life of ours. Possibly I exaggerate this meaning. But you shall judge for yourself if you care to read:

What the Admiral Told Me.

When I was in command of the *North Carolina* in 190–, we were sent on a friendly visit to Japan. Of course we were well entertained with public receptions and private feasts. The Japanese understand beautifully how to do these things. Even when they courteously adopt Occidental customs, their imitation is creditable and pleasant. But when they know and like you well enough to do things in their own quaint and dainty way, it is much better.

There was an unofficial banquet for half a dozen of us officers at the Maple Club in one of the Tokyo parks. A Geisha entertainment of the refined type adorned the feast. After dinner the flower-like girls pleased us with a few of their dances—more like brief pantomime plays than our idea of dancing, which seems to be a mechanical repetition of set motions without meaning under the tyrannical noise of a barbaric band. But this performance of a people whom we call in our ignorant pride, "little brown monkeys," was vastly more civilized than our ball-room gyrations or cabaret convulsions. It was graceful, intelligent, full of poetry and sentiment.

Evidently it made a great impression on my fourth officer, Lieutenant C——, from Charleston, South Carolina. You really ought to have known that young man in order to appreciate, or perhaps even to believe, this story. He was a thoroughbred of old Huguenot stock; quick-minded, clever, highly sensitive, devout, and extremely imaginative. His impulses were lively but his sense of duty was strong. He was a first-rate officer, with firm principles under quiet manners, and an independent spirit which obeyed orders promptly as long as they came with authority. But one always had a feeling that if he were released, or released himself, from that authority, there was no telling what C——'s queer combination of a passionate love of beauty with an extreme conscientiousness might not make him do.

Well, as I said, he was fascinated by this decorously beautiful performance at the Maple Club.

The brilliant joyous garments, the pliant gestures, the waving fans and woven paces, seemed to create an atmosphere of charm which carried him away from himself and from the rest of us. His attention was centred on a certain little girl about ten or eleven years old who appeared to be the attendant and pupil of the leading Geisha. Around this statelier person the exquisite small creature danced like a sunbeam around a tall purple foxglove. Her glossy black hair, her lustrous almond eyes, her tiny mouth curved in an unconscious smile, rose from a shimmering gold-thread robe embroidered with silver flowers. Every motion of her body was light and glad as if she were in an ecstasy.

"Look at that little one, sir," C—— whispered to me. "Isn't she perfect? She's like a child fairy. She's the very bud of the East. The others are sometimes a bit ponderous. But that ray of sunlight reminds me of a verse from the Old Testament, —'a garment of praise for the spirit of heaviness.'"

Of course such high-flown sentimental talk made me a little uneasy about C——, knowing his temperament as I did. But I must say his conduct was faultless. He went back to the ship with the rest of us, and during the remainder of our stay in Yokohama, so far as I know, he made no effort to find out anything about his "bud of the East." But I have no doubt he carried a pretty vivid image of her in his romantic heart. It did not interfere at all with his exemplary doing of his duty.

In a short time he got his promotion as Lieutenant-Commander and was sent back to Japan and Korea on a special, confidential mission. He was most successful and brought home a valuable report. But his work was not recognized by the Government, nor even visibly appreciated by the Department. His sensitive nature was deeply grieved and wounded by this apparent neglect. He had not yet learned that to carry on a life of service in the Navy a man at times must have a patient temper and a bit of alligator-skin over his heart. C—— did not have this armor-plating. He felt that he was pierced in a vital spot, and his conscience told him that he must resign his commission. I did not agree with him, but that was no reason why I should blame him or question his sincere patriotism.

In his disappointment he turned more intensely than ever to religion. He wanted to Americanize the world by pacific methods, by teaching Christianity in that particular form and garb which appealed to him most. So he entered an institution for training missionary teachers. His natural gifts carried him quickly through the course, and he obtained a place in a famous school in a certain ancient city of Japan—a city which I will not name, for obvious reasons.

Meantime his beautiful "bud of the East,"—O Yei Tama,—was of course unfolding and growing up. She came of a good Samurai family. Her father's bankruptcy had forced her, in a daughter's devotion, to turn toward the profession of a Geisha. But in some way or other he had recovered most of his property and, perhaps in gratitude for this, had become a convert to Christianity and had entered the lovely Yei Tama in the great school to which C—— was preparing to come as a missionary teacher. There she was when he arrived. After some observation and inquiry he identified this favorite pupil and assistant teacher with the fairy child who had danced into his heart at the Maple Club eight years ago.

Imagine the situation ! Yes, it was quite dramatic,— in the moving-picture style,—but it really happened.

You foresee how the story goes on. C—— discovers that the seed of love has not been withered by absence, but has taken deep hold on him, and now grows up and flowers wonderfully. Yei Tama is captivated by her handsome and dignified teacher, listens enchanted to the lover's tale of his long-ago dreams of her, yields to his pleading, responds to his ideal passion, and gladly becomes his wife. C—— has a modest fortune of his own; buys a pretty bungalow in a suburb at the foot of the Sacred Mountain; surrounds it with a garden in the fashion of Tea Neck, New Jersey; furnishes it in American style; and enters into matrimonial bliss. And that is that!

But the part of the play that seems to me most interesting and significant,—the part that nearly turned it from a genteel comedy of love into a sorrowful tragedy of despair,—that part came a little later.

C——, you must know, had the idiotic but popular notion that the only way for East and West ever to meet is for East to become absolutely and entirely West. If that were so, what would be the use of their meeting? It would be nothing but a repetition, a mirror-meeting, a mere increase of something of which we already have perhaps a little too much. Wouldn't it be better if West, bestowing gifts, could enjoy something that East has to give? Couldn't Christianity be as real and true in Oriental dress, and manners, and ways of reasoning and speaking, as it is in the modes of Boston and Baltimore? Certainly it began East of Suez. You can't really understand the Bible unless you remember that it employs Oriental methods of thought and expression,—poetical illustrations instead of logical arguments,—parables and symbols instead of definitions. I am sure our Lord Jesus, and His fishermen-disciples, and the sisters Mary and Martha, used costumes and customs that belonged to East much more than to West. At least, that is what I think about it.

But my intense young friend C—— did not think that way. He believed that the mission of America was to make the world one hundred per cent American. He thought that the only way to Christianize people was to make them dress and act like the folks at a Consecration Conference in Soda Springs, Arkansas. Of course he held that religion is a life in the spirit; but he had the idea that a good way to promote it is to work from the outside inward, to reshape the dress and manners of a convert in order to conform the soul to the fashion which C——

approved. He tried this method on his fair Yei Tama with lamentable results.

You may remember that the modes of feminine apparel which Paris sent to New York at the beginning of the twentieth century, and which gradually filtered out to missionary circles, were not of an ideal beauty. They compressed a woman's form like the steel sides of a destroyer. They promoted ungainly protuberances at bow and stern. They used a superfluous amount of costly material to no good purpose, and they simply rioted in unnecessary rigging of streamers, knots, and frills.

Some such attire as this,—you understand that I am no expert in describing the details,—the infatuated C—— provided for the beauteous Yei Tama. He insisted that she should wear it as an outward and visible sign of her conversion and Americanization. She yielded to his desire with the sweet pliancy of a true daughter of Nippon. But she knew right well that these clothes did not suit her at all. They made her look like a badly stuffed German doll, with humps where there should have been hollows, and angles where there should have been flowing lines. A woman, East or West, knows when her dress is unbecoming, and she does not like it at all.

It makes her awkward and unhappy, and she can't help showing it.

But there were other changes even more irksome on which the infatuated uplifter of womanhood insisted mildly but firmly,—changes in manners and habits. The quaint appealing Japanese salutation to a welcome stranger must give way to the stiff American nod, or the pump-like handshaking. The pretty tripping walk must be transformed into a stately stride. She ought to be more dignified, more reserved, more like the wife of an American missionary teacher. The easy idle talk of birds and flowers should be replaced by serious conversation on politics and theology. The little dance-steps *à l'impréviste* that moved her feet when she was merry should be given up. The long-handled guitar should be laid aside. The small curious songs that came to her lips so easily when her feelings were moved should be repressed. They were too emotional, not appropriate to her position. They belonged to the past which was abandoned when she embraced Christianity and her husband.

While the conscientious idiot was painfully and vainly engaged in trying to remake the woman God had given him, Yei Tama was uncomfortable and sad, in spite of her abiding love. So was he. He felt that his efforts were unsuccessful. His woman was not really changed; she was only obedient. This troubled him greatly. He did not blame her; he blamed himself for his failure to accomplish the impossible. He began to believe that she would never change to his pattern. All that he had done thus far was to suppress the very charm which had first drawn him to her. What was left? Nothing but an obviously poor imitation of the good women whom he had approved but who had never charmed him.

Was his marriage then a mistake? Had he put his head into a wreath of flowers only to find that it hid a yoke and a heavy burden? You see at this time he thought, like some reformers, mainly of himself. He told me so afterward. He did not inquire about Yei Tama's marriage,—whether that also had been a mistake? Whether she too had a yoke and burden to bear?

Affairs came to a head at a little dinner to which C—— invited my wife and me with a few other American friends who were visiting the ancient Japanese city a year or so after his wedding. He wanted us to see his new house and wife. He had the hospitable instincts of a Southerner,—at least on the material side. The dinner was properly cooked and decorously served. The house was neat, orderly, and dull. But on the convivial side,—the side of joyous fellowship,—the feast was what the boys call "a washout." There was nothing in it.

C—— sat at one end of the table, constrained, apprehensive, glancing at his wife to see how she acquitted herself in her new position, and listening with one ear to her conversation even while other people talked to him. Yei Tama sat at the other end of the table, anxious, embarrassed, trying to catch a look of approval in her husband's eyes, but never for a moment at ease or happy.

Her natural beauty was entirely obscured by her fatal dress. I did my best to enliven the occasion. Others tried to make a little breeze of joy in talk. Mrs. Leventritt ventured one of her most lively stories. The poor young hostess did not know whether to laugh or look shocked. C—— did not help her. He was like a watchful graven image. I could see people thinking, "Now what the deuce induced C——?"

After the depressing dinner the other guests drove home to the hotel. But I kept one of the jinrikishas waiting and stayed on for a little while to have a talk with Yei Tama. She was very frank and charming with me, and I got from her a good idea of the state of affairs. I took an old man's privilege of giving her a word of friendly advice,—not strictly orthodox, I fear, but good enough as sailing orders in an emergency. C—— came in from the veranda, where he had been gloomily smoking his pipe, and asked if I would take a short moonlight walk with him. I agreed readily, for there was another word of unorthodox advice that I wanted to give to him personally.

We went along the road about a quarter of a mile in silence. Then we took a path across a field and turned into one of those miraculously beautiful forest glens which furrow the side of the Sacred Mountain. You know the sort of thing,—tall solemn evergreens like columns in a cathedral; luxuriant ferns and undergrowth faintly glistening where a stray moonbean pierced the green roof; a small brook, a mere rivulet, tinkling and purling down the glen; and where it made a turn, a smooth, open place carpeted with moss. Here we sat down on two big rocks and my young friend unburdened his heart to me.

He told of his preposterous intentions, desires, and efforts in regard to his wife. He was very much depressed, evidently at the end of his rope. Of course I can give you only the gist of our talk.

"I felt it my duty both as a Christian and as an American," he said at last, "to bring her into an entirely new life in which she would become an altogether different woman. But I have failed miserably. I have killed the thing I loved. But I cannot create the thing I planned. What is left for me? How can I get out of this hole? I have thought of suicide, but that would be impossible for a man of our family. It would be dishonor. Divorce? There is no ground for it, and besides, we old South Carolinians do not believe in divorce; it seems to us disgraceful. I don't know what to do. Can you, sir, out of your long experience of life advise me?"

"I surely can," was my answer. "The advice will be of service to you if you take it. It is all very well for you to be one hundred per cent American and Christian. But there is no need of your being also a —— fool. It's the doctrine of America that every person has a right to 'life, liberty, and the pursuit of happiness.' Why not grant this to your wife? Christianity tells us that we may not judge one another. Why not apply this to your wife? You have no commission to make her over again. That is God's affair, if he thinks it best; and I don't believe he will, because he has already made her very lovely

and good enough for any man. What you have
promised to do is to love, honor, and cherish her as
she is. Try that, and see how it works.

"My young friend, half the troubles in the world,
and a good many of the wars, come from the insane
desire of some people to compel others to conform
to their notions of the true, the beautiful, and the
good in every detail of life. That is impossible without force, and force cannot change nature. Only
grace can do that.

"Your thinking of suicide or divorce is absurd,
overstrained, neurotic. Your saying that you have
'killed the thing you loved' is ridiculous, a silly
quotation from some pessimistic novel. You certainly have not killed her because she is very much
alive, and she loves you and you love her. Do you
know, I told her what you said at the Maple Club
long ago about her 'garment of praise,' and she was
immensely pleased. Then I asked her if she could
put it on, or something like it, and come up here with
her maid to fetch us home. She said she would not be
afraid, except of displeasing you. I assured her that
would be all right. Look, if I am not mistaken, there
she is now, coming up through the forest."

Among the dark-red trunks of the pine-trees,

through the shadows and the pools of moonlight, holding her long-necked guitar and stepping light and shy as a fawn, came the lovely Yei Tama. She dropped her dark cloak and showed her robe of soft, clear yellow like an evening primrose; round her waist was a broad obi of old rose richly embroidered with gold and silver; and beneath the robe, a kerchief of white silk covered her breast. As she walked she sang to her guitar the "Song of the Cherry Blossom," and when she came to the space of open ground covered with moss she did a few steps and gestures of that graceful dance. Her sandalled feet shone on the green like pearls in a cup of malachite. Then she dropped her guitar, ran to her husband, and threw her bare arms around his neck in silence.

"O Yei," he said, "dearest Yei Tama, God has given you back to me. I love you just as you are, in your garment of praise. Are you all mine this way?"

"Every way," said she.

At this point I thought it best to leave them and scramble down the glen, following the maid, for I knew that my dear wife would be waiting for me at the hotel.

THE SILVER DOCTOR

THE SILVER DOCTOR

I

THE CASE

GEORGE BREWSTER was one of those rare physicians who know the limitations of physic, and the potencies of mental treatment administered by a doctor who is fortunate enough to have a mind. He used medicines of course: tonics with discretion, sedatives with wisdom, narcotics with parsimony. When needed, he would give a whisper to the sleepy liver, a soother to the irritated lungs, a calmer to the jumpy heart.

"If Nature has provided specifics for certain organs," he said, "there is no reason why we should not employ them to help us out. It reduces friction. But what I really try to get into shape is not only the organ, but also the organist. Do that, and you're pretty sure of better music."

Of the knife, (which he could use at need with great skill,) he thought chiefly as a first aid to the injured or the last call in an emergency. He was no indiscriminate carver.

He considered it well for a normal man, barring internal and external accidents, to carry to his coffin all that he had in his cradle; and if possible, a few extra things, such as teeth and hair.

These views were regarded as antiquated and eccentric among the higher specialists. But they did not prevent him from having a great many patients who swore by him, not at him, and for whom as a rule he did exceedingly well.

Among them an aggravating and disappointing favorite was Van Buren Gilbert. He was a Wall Street man in the early thirties who had made an amazing success in his business at a frightful cost to his health. Close application had worn him down to a fine fragile point, like an over-sharpened pencil. Press on it a shade too hard and it will snap off. The strenuous forms of exercise which he practised, —court tennis and polo,—wore him out more than they refreshed him. He was so keen to win that he got little fun out of the games. At last they became impossible for his shaken nerves, and he went on the melancholy "invalid list."

He *really* had chronic dyspepsia, insomnia, and intercostal neuralgia. He *imagined* that he had successively (1) heart disease, (2) galloping consumption, (3) cancer, (4) paresis. None of these things actually ailed him; but imagining them made him frightfully gloomy and cross. He was simply, (or, rather, complicatedly,) suffering from an intense neurasthenia,—that many-sided play-actor among human ailments.

But it was real enough, if you come to that, and unless he could be delivered from it, it might easily bring him to the insane asylum, or leave him to walk the world as a *malade imaginaire*, a walking indigestion.

Doctor Brewster, who had been an intimate friend of his since college days, sized up the case promptly, and treated it patiently for over six months, doing all he could to relieve the distressing symptoms with appropriate remedies and diet. The sick man simply *would not* get well. He was sent to a sanitarium, and kicked. He was brought home to his own house, and languished. Every morning between two and three he thought he was dying. Every afternoon about five he was really quite low.

"George," he complained, "you don't seem able to do much for me. Have I got to die at thirty-four? That's rather hard lines."

"Look here, Van," said Brewster, whose patience

was worn out, "there's nothing at all the matter with you except a bad case of what Mrs. Malaprop called 'nervous prosperity.' There isn't a single organic lesion in your body, so far as I can find out. But your mind is split between pious self-pity and profane rebellion. You can be cured; but nobody can do anything for you as long as you keep on saying 'damn! damn! damn!' inside of yourself all the time."

Gilbert grinned, for this struck him as funny.

"Well," he said, "you swore first, anyhow. Now quit it, and tell me what you want me to do. I know I've been rather a beast, awfully hard to handle. But I'll be good and do whatever you tell me without a single damn."

"It is very simple. The best thing for you is a water-cure,—but not at one of those sodden hotel-hospitals which the British call a 'hydro.' That would finish you,—too many self-sick people hanging around telling each other about their symptoms. What you need is water *au naturel*. There's a wonderful little spring up in the Alleghany Mountains,—not known to the public yet, never bottled,—but it's a specific for just such cases as yours. It flows into a beautiful brook called the Brightwater, which has two or three fine swimming-holes in it. On the bank of the stream there's an old-fashioned inn named after it; in fact, the annex almost hangs over the water, so that you can hear it singing and rippling down all day,—and all night, too, if you could only stay awake, which you can't. There are some pretty trout in the brook; well-educated fish; you must try to catch them."

"But, George, that would be too violent exercise for me. You know I can't walk a couple of blocks without a palpitation. Besides, I haven't fished since I was a boy in college. It seems childish."

"That's just the trouble with you. You've discarded all the nice, simple, silly things that make life pleasant and wholesome, and given yourself soul and body to making money. Well, you've made enough to last the rest of your days; yes, and longer than that if you don't pull out of this sickness. Use some of your money, it will only take a little, to help you away from the misery you are in now."

"But my interests, doctor, my investments; they are important. I must stay here to keep my eye on them."

"Much good your eye is now! Besides, what's the matter with your friends' eyes? You've retired from the firm, but your old partners are good business men; you can trust them better than you can trust yourself in your present condition. Give Jimmy Hope your power of attorney. Cut all the strings of business behind you, and 'hie to the mountains, my own stricken deer.' "

"But the journey, George, the journey in the train will be too much for me. I can't stand it. And there will be no doctor at this place in the mountains,— whatever you call it."

"Pish! and posh! You are not going in a train, you are going in your own absurdly luxurious car,— a lovely drive across Jersey and through the Water Gap. Your man Jenkins is a first-rate chauffeur and a good nurse in emergency. There's an excellent country doctor half a mile from Brightwater. But you won't need a doctor, or a nurse. What you'll need in a couple of weeks is a gillie!

"Remember, now, two birch-bark cupfuls of that spring-water every morning before breakfast, and a daily plunge in one of those pools as soon as the weather gets warm enough. I'll send you around a fly-rod and all the other tackle this afternoon. Off you go to Brightwater to-morrow. So long, and good luck to your fishing!"

The packing of two suitcases and a steamer trunk was deftly done by Jenkins, while Gilbert looked on, mildly excited. The fishing things, including a pair of waterproof waders and brogans, were sent by the doctor. Gilbert eyed them with curiosity and contempt.

"Oh, put 'em in if you like. They'll be about as much use to me as skates to a one-legged man. But I don't want to hurt the doctor's feelings."

Jenkins said "Yessir" and obeyed the doctor's instructions. He also prepared a sort of couch in the back part of the limousine, for Gilbert insisted that he was too feeble to sit up. A luncheon-basket he fleered at; but Jenkins packed one with a tiny silver flask, a thermos bottle of clear coffee, and plenty of thin chicken sandwiches. Through the grinding tangle of New York and the dingy, clanging streets of Hoboken, the invalid reclined and grunted. But when the car swept across the Newark meadows and climbed the Orange Hills, he began to sit up and take notice.

"Jenkins, it seems to me this air is a little better, easier to breathe. What?"

"Yessir, more like country air, sir. Much healthier, *I* think."

"How about that front seat? It rides smoother, doesn't it? My back is almost broken with this bumping. This beastly couch is too short. What?"

"Yessir. It's much smoother here. You can get a look in at the country, too. Seems a bit like Dorset, if you'll excuse me saying so. I'll arrange this seat, sir."

There is nothing spectacular about the scenery of Northern New Jersey, but it is lovely and pleasant, —a consoling landscape, full of friendly charm. The hills were discreetly folded about the valleys with a protective air. The meadows and broad fields where the early ploughman was tracing his furrows had an expectant look, eager for spring. In damp places the grass was greening, and the pussy-willows were showing their fur. The forests were not primeval, but they were kind and cheerful, evidently getting ready for a festival. Bright leaves of May-apple spread over the carpet of withered foliage on the ground, tassels and delicate embroideries of poplar and maple and birch filled the upper air. In the towns of Montclair and Caldwell and Dover and Netcong the yellow Forsythia gilded the cottage yards. The little rivers were full of water making a cheerful noise unto the Lord. At a friendly corner on the bank of the Musconetcong, soothed and sub-consciously invigorated, Gilbert spoke up more like a man than he had spoken for many months.

"Jenkins, I saw you hide a lunch-basket in the car. What about it? What's in it?"

"That's what I say, sir. We can find out if we open it. A try would do no harm. We'll pull out of the road a bit here and sit in the car while we eat, sir, if that would suit you."

"Better get out," said Gilbert, much to the chauffeur's surprise. "It will do us good to stretch our legs. Those rocks look dry. Let's see if we can find a soft side on them. What?"

The contents of the little silver flask, mixed with *aqua pura* from a spring, made two good appetizers; the thin sandwiches went "down the red lane"; the coffee was hot and heartening; a short smoke afterward seemed to fill the bill completely.

The car rolled smoothly on over the hills and down the long grade to Delaware; across the bridge above the broad, brimful river; between the steep mountains of the Water Gap; through the town of Strouds-burg, and up the winding valley of Brodhead's Creek. As the sun declined, the hills seemed to come nearer, dark in the west but still brightly glowing in the east.

Ancient mill and ruined tannery, yellow farmhouse and red barn looked larger in the half-day. The lilac twilight was weaving its diaphanous veil over the countryside as the automobile turned up the Brightwater Valley, crossed the stream, and arrived at the old-fashioned, rambling, wooden Inn.

By this time Gilbert was depressed again. He was tired, low in his mind, nervous at finding himself in a strange, far-off place, though in the morning he would have sworn there was nothing he wanted so much as to get away from the stale luxuries of his bachelor apartment on Park Avenue.

But the welcome of John Woodman and Lottie his wife, who ran the Inn, was so warm and quiet; the supper of scrambled eggs and bacon, with fresh asparagus on toast, was so satisfying; the rooms in the annex overhanging the stream were so clean and simple, with good beds and plenty of blankets for a cool night, that Gilbert's jumpy heart was reassured and quieted. He began to feel a sense of something that the Scotch call "couthy" in the place.

"Jenkins," he said, "this is not so bad, after all. Lay out my things and help me off with my boots, will you? Your room is just back of this; so if I call or knock on the wall you can come in at once. No,

I don't think I'll take my 'sleeper' to-night. Don't feel as if I needed it.—Absolutely nothing on my mind except sleep."

"Right you are, sir," said the wise Jenkins. "And if I was you, I'd drop off all those medicines as fast as I could. In the long run you just get dependent on 'em,—kind of slavery, if you see what I mean. I'll be handy, sir, and with you in a minute if you call,—but I don't think you will. It's a fine cool night for sleeping and the sound of that brook is kind of soothing. Good night, sir."

"Thank you. Remember to lay out my knickers and heavy boots in the morning. But don't call me if you value your life."

He sat on his bed for a few minutes, wondering what to-morrow would be like in this strange place, listening to the water-music and the faint, monotonous chant of a whippoorwill far down the valley. Then he felt chilly, turned in between the coarse linen sheets under the warm blankets, and before he knew it had rolled over the edge of consciousness into the timeless depths of perfect sleep.

II

THE TREATMENT

He was awakened next morning by the impetuous carolling of two rowdy robins who were putting up a residence in the Virginia creeper that curtained the veranda of the annex. They worked like beavers and sang like exhilarated college students. Between their bursts of headlong music Gilbert could hear the discreet, tuneful voice of a little song-sparrow from a bush in the meadow below. His watch showed the hour as six-thirty.

"Real time," he said, "not the fool time that silly men have invented to persuade themselves to get up an hour earlier by telling a lie about it. Just like most of our asinine civilization,—call a lie a social convention, and it goes."

He knocked on the wall for Jenkins, put on his gray Norfolk suit and thick boots, and went downstairs to inquire about the wonder-working spring.

"It's just beside the annex," said John Woodman. "Go down those stone steps into that kind of a shallow well and you'll find it."

"Doctor Brewster said something about using a birch-bark cup. He seemed to think the water would do me more good that way."

John laughed.

"That's an old hobby of the doctor's. He always makes his own cups; pins 'em together with wooden pegs and a cleft stick for a handle. But there's a gourd dipper down there now; guess that'll do you just as much good."

The five stone steps led down into a circular walled enclosure, from the bottom of which a gnarled apple-tree stretched its arms into the air. At the foot of the tree was the spring, gushing out beneath a stratum of the mother rock. Through the crystal water you could see tiny cones of white sand dancing and disappearing and dancing again where the invisible current came in. Gilbert drank two gourdfuls with delight, hung the dipper on its nail again and went up to breakfast.

There were three ladies in the room,—bird-struck maiden ladies who came up to the Inn every year to watch and annotate the warblers, vireos, and thrushes; for Brightwater lies on a through line of the semiannual migration. To these ladies the newcomer was duly presented by Mrs. Woodman. There were also two disciples of Izaak Walton, members of a little company formed to protect the stream from rustic poachers and the Inn from urban innovators.

These brothers of the angle made Gilbert welcome, (Doctor Brewster, an old member, had written to announce his patient's coming,) invited him to share the dish of trout they had caught the day before, provided him with a license and a ticket for the waters of the Preserve, and fell into talk about fish and fishing. They compared rods and reels, fly-books and leaders, and disputed the relative merits of a March Brown and a Cowdung fly. Gilbert was modest and rather silent, but much entertained to see how earnest middle-aged men could be about an idle pastime. They offered to show him the stream. One of them was going to fish up, where it was more rough and brushy; the other was going to fish down, where the water was open. They invited him to choose.

"Thank you very much," he said, "but I'm only a novice, I don't want to bother either of you. Besides, you see I'm an invalid,—bad heart,—fishing would be too hard work for me. Later perhaps, in the summer, I can do it."

In the morning he went up-stream with the bird-struck maiden ladies to learn about the different kinds of warblers. The Blackburnian seemed to him the most brilliant, but the little Parula with its tiny sapphire necklace and its soft dreamy song was more attractive. In the afternoon he napped a little, and toward sunset walked alone down-stream. In the short pools among the pussy-willows in the horse-pasture he saw plenty of small trout rising. Following the winding path through the rhododendrons, he came to a long pool with a big rock in the middle; and there, in smooth shallow water at the foot, was a larger trout, at least ten inches long, leisurely sucking in the floating flies and leaving a round "kiss" on the surface of the water as each morsel disappeared. He began to wonder whether he could possibly catch that fish, and whether up-stream or down-stream would be the better way to approach it, and how soon he would be well enough to try his hand at the fishing.

That evening there was a mild rubber of Bridge. By the time Gilbert was half-way across it, he was sleepy; and at half after nine (real time) he excused himself and went up to bed.

"How does this place please you, Jenkins?" he asked as he was undressing.

"Looks to me like a little bit of all right, sir, if

you'll pardon me saying so. That home-cured bacon reminds me of my old uncle in Dorset. It almost brings the tears to my eyes."

"What do you think of the people? I don't mean the boarders, but the people who run the house."

"First-rate, sir; so natural and friendly,—'common' *they* call it. If you'll excuse me, sir, that's what they called *you*, meaning it complimentary, of course. Mr. Woodman, he used to be watchman on the stream, a 'keeper,' as we say in the old country. And Mrs. Woodman, she was a farmer's daughter with a good schooling. They had a little money laid by, and they were terrible fond of each other. So they joined hands and took a chance on running this place. The fishing gentlemen that come here helped 'em. Good sort of people, sir, fishermen generally, easy-going and generous, don't you think?"

"Yes, I suppose you can say that much of anglers without exaggeration. They're usually easy-going. In fact I've almost made up my mind to try being one, for a little while at any rate. It's a childish sport, utterly unreasonable, working all day for a few small fishes that you could buy for less money than your tackle costs. It is a form of lunacy, but there's something soothing about it, so I am going to try it. Good night, call me at six-thirty standard. Those robins may forget."

For three or four days the invalid continued this pleasant loafing life, drinking his two gourds of the miraculous spring-water each morning and growing steadier and stronger every day. When it rained he had a box of old books, like "Lorna Doone," "A Princess of Thule," "Redgauntlet," "A Maid of Sker," "White Heather," which Brewster had sent up to entertain him. There were a few good new ones like Buchan's "John McNab," and Donn Byrne's "Hangman's House." All of them had something about sport in them, and none of them dabbled in morbid sex-psychology.

The avian amateurs taught him to distinguish five of the fifty kinds of warblers and how to tell a red-eyed vireo from a Pennsylvania vireo. The anglers went over his fly-book carefully with him, and pointed out the flies to which the trout of the region were supposed to be most susceptible,—Queen of the Water, Royal Coachman, Hare's Ear, Red Hackle, Black Gnat, and so on. Over the Seth Green they fell into dispute, the one alleging that it was a "worthless concoction," the other affirming that on certain days it was "the most killing fly on the stream." About the value of the Hackstaff they were agreed.

'It was invented right here on this brook, by one of our old members. You see it is all gray, with a yellow bunch at the end of the body. That represents the sac of eggs which the natural fly is about to deposit on the water. On a good day, warm and slightly cloudy, no normal trout can resist it. But there are no Hackstaffs in your book. Let us give you half a dozen."

Jenkins' favorable verdict on the character of anglers was confirmed. Gilbert's secret interest and ambition increased. On the fifth day after his arrival at the water-cure he put on his waders and brogans, tightened up his courage and his belt, jointed his rod and rigged a cast of flies, slung a creel over his shoulder, and started out, almost surreptitiously, to try his luck up-stream.

At first he went as delicately as Agag. His feelings were uncertain and tremulous. Suppose he should have one of his fainting turns. Suppose he should fall on the rocks and break his leg, or tumble face down in the stream and be drowned.

From these morbid thoughts the vireos and warblers fluttering through the thickets diverted his mind. The trout that he saw in the pools allured and irritated him. Why did they dart away as he approached? Why couldn't he lightly drop his flies over them before they vanished? Why did he get hooked up so often in the branches of overhanging trees? He lost three leaders and seven flies in that absurd way. He was not going to let this silly pastime get the better of him. He was determined to learn how to do it. So he waded and cast resolutely until at last he hooked and landed an extremely ignorant seven-inch trout. With this he went home, very tired and late to lunch, but secretly elated because he had not been entirely "skunked."

The next day he went down-stream and did better, —three trout in the creel and only two leaders left in trees. The day after, the balance between profit and loss was still further improved: debit, one cast of flies; credit, four fish, one of them nine inches long. He also made the acquaintance of two affable rose-breasted grosbeaks who were locating their summer cottage in a young birch-tree. Thus

"Happily the days of Thalaba went by," each bringing some new small adventure, some livelier sensation of well-being. His excursions on the brook grew longer and longer, leading him up beyond the deserted mill, and down beyond the Woodmans' wood-lot, and Billy Lerns' spring-house, and the Snaky Glen, and the Naiad's Elbow, a good three miles away. From these more distant expeditions he had the car to bring him home. Once he drove over to Pocono to explore that creek, and once to Paradise Valley to fish the brook beside which Joe Jefferson wrote the play of Rip van Winkle. But no other stream comforted and pleased him like the Brightwater. It seemed to flow through his heart.

New people came to the Inn, but Gilbert kept company chiefly with his first friends and chatted much with the Woodmans. Lottie told him curious tales of the Pennsylvania Dutch who inhabited the region roundabout. They had "powwows,"—secret, traditional charms,—infallible against certain diseases and calamities.

"Grandmother believed in those things," said Lottie, "but mother was a healthy doubter. There was an old woman who had a powwow for rheumatism. She used it on Billy Lerns and he got better. But *I* guess it was because he gave up drinking 'Jersey lightning.'"

Of course Gilbert had his relapses, his bad days, when his heart fluttered or his imaginary cancer gave him a pain in the stomach. But by refraining from conversation about these things he seemed to reduce their importance and lessen their reality. The strenuous world of Wall Street, the jazzing world of the Great White Way, receded from him; the little world around this valley-dimple on the flank of Mount Pocono became more real and intimate. He had roadside talks with the farmers ploughing or planting their stony fields. He observed the curious contents of the cottages turned inside out by the convulsion of spring cleaning; chairs and tables piled up on the porches, carpets and bed-quilts hanging on the fences. He noted also the form and walk of the young women and girls who hung out the wash in the yard, or strolled along the road on their way to school; their firm necks, their swinging shoulders, their broad hips, their easy stride. What a pity that such creatures should be withered into the stiff and sallow anatomy of some of the farm-wives.

In the bird-ladies at the Inn he saw new and attractive features: the silky softness of Miss Simpson's abundant gray hair, the fugitive dimple and the pearly teeth in Miss Lowman's smile, the kindness of Miss Frame's brown eyes behind her big round spectacles.

It is an odd thing, (but I have frequently observed it,) that when a man has passed through a severe illness and begins to feel the rising tide of health again, the first sign of it is a heightened susceptibility to womanly charms. You remember Henry Drowne made his hasty marriage shortly after his recovery from typhoid fever. How many men have wedded their nurses, often happily, but sometimes otherwise! Only two months after he got up from a double pneumonia, Jack Barnes discovered his priceless wife in a schoolmistress.

Perhaps it is a natural effect of the returning vigor of manhood. Perhaps it is the result of enforced reflection on the brevity and uncertainty of life and a fear that it may be cut short before it has yielded the best it has to give,—which best, according to Robert Browning and others, is Love with a capital letter. (See "Love among the Ruins," "Meeting at Night," and other poems.) Perhaps it is a practical deduction from that truth which the great Jehovah put into nine short words in Eden: "It is not good for man to be alone." Who can tell the psychological reason and the physical cause? It often happens; that is all we can say. And it happened to Gilbert.

He was certainly not meditating matrimony. There was nothing in the bird-struck ladies at the Inn, or in the restless "flappers" among the new guests, to suggest that solemn thought. Nor did he recall with pleasure the memory of his few amatory adventures in college and afterward, and wish to repeat them. They were as dusty as an ancient masked-ball costume, hanging for years forgotten in a closet. It was a long time since "the ever-womanly" had played any part in his tense life of financial success and vital failure. He was now simply and half-unconsciously returning to normality; considering whether the world had not somewhere in its vast population a complete comrade to give him for his life-journey, which was apparently to continue longer than he had thought; wondering whether by some good fortune he might not find "that not impossible she," whom he could make entirely happy and with whom he could realize full happiness. In short, while he loafed and fished and made friends with nature, he was ripening for real love.

His step grew firm and springy as he followed the angler's path or waded the stream. His eyes brightened; his face took on a wholesome brown; the plaintive down-creases at the corners of his mouth disappeared. His angling improved daily; he could cast more accurately and strike a rising fish more quickly. He took a fancy to the lower reaches of the stream, where it cuts through the big Red Rock. There the pools are deeper, the trout larger. One afternoon he came back from there with a proud basket: eleven trout over ten inches in length, and one,—well, let us say, for the sake of brevity, a foot long. It was the catch of the season.

He resolved to go there again very early the next morning, taking a cold breakfast with him in the car, and having a plunge in one of the pools before he ate. The car rolling through a world of auroral beauty, stopped in the road high on the hillside and let him out. He made his way down by the side of a gardenful of peonies and iris, blooming around a comfortable, well-kept house, and entered the thick woods which lay between it and the brook. Unjointed rod in hand, he walked carefully and noiselessly among the dark hemlocks, the smooth beeches, the laurel thickets. Coming to the water's edge, but still hidden by the bushes, he looked across the pool and saw the loveliest vision of his life.

A Naiad of the stream, or was it the Dryad of a silver birch-tree, was at her bath. A light loin-cloth of blue girdled her hips. Her snowy arms and breasts glistened against the dark green of the rhododendrons on the opposite bank; her footing gleamed white through the crystal water above the red rock which bottomed the pool. Her face was fairer than the sun, clearer than the moon; her hair of russet gold was a crown upon her head; her eyes were bluer than fringed gentians. Motionless and silent she stood, as one in a dream, the clear drops falling from her arms and sides, one hand on her bosom, her look fixed upon the flowing water as if she searched for something in the cool depths.

The man, (no prying Actæon by nature,) was entranced and overwhelmed by the beauty of the apparition. It seemed supernatural. Yet he knew it was real.

"Good God," he whispered to himself, "I must get away from this as quickly and quietly as I can. If she knew that I was here, she would be so frightened and ashamed! It would be terrible,—I couldn't stand it. Lord help me out of this thicket without cracking one dead branch."

He crept through the wood, made a wide circle around the house, climbed the hill, found his car waiting, and climbed in, without having set up his rod or wet a line. Jenkins was astonished.

"Was anything wrong with the stream, sir? Did you find some one fishing there ahead of you?"

"Yes,—that is, no,—it's of no consequence,—drive home,—I'll get my breakfast at the Inn."

That meal was a spare and silent one, so far as Gilbert was concerned. He paid no attention to it. His mind was down the brook.

III

THE RELAPSE

The day which had opened so brightly with a rosy sunrise turned dark in the forenoon, and by eleven o'clock a drizzling rain set in. It changed to a steady downpour by three and the mountains hid their heads in cloud. Gilbert's spirits sank with the barometer. His heart tried to turn somersaults. His pulse fluttered awhile and then hammered hard. He was sure his blood-pressure had gone far above normal. He accused himself of low conduct, ungentlemanly spying on a helpless girl, mean and cowardly behavior. He could feel something gnawing in his left side,—probably that old cancer getting to work again after a short rest. How treacherous these diseases were! He was horribly depressed and went to bed before supper, after sending Jenkins to the post-office with a telegram for the doctor.

"*Much worse please come at once if possible.* VAN."

The answer was received in a couple of hours.

"*Not worse you only think so coming to-morrow Sunday noon.* GEORGE."

This bucked the patient up a little, but the effect was not lasting. It was a hard night, especially for Jenkins. One sleeping-draught, a long massage, another sleeping-draught, a mustard foot-bath to draw the blood from the head, two powders,—all without effect. Then a stiff, hot lemonade did the necessary business, brought on a wholesome sweat and a blessed forgetfulness of self. His only dreams were rather pleasant; very brief, no conclusions, only vanishings.

Gilbert slept very late. The rain had put a damper on the rowdy robins. The first sound that he heard was the louder song of the full brook, rejoicing down toward the Red Rock. His watch showed that it was past ten o'clock. Incredible that time should still be going on as if nothing had happened. He called for a cup of strong tea and two slices of toast. He filled his favorite pipe and lit it. Then the doctor came in, fresh and moist after his ride from Pocono Station in a touring-car through the rain.

"Hallo, old man, how are you? Much better, I see. You must have gained ten pounds. Healthy color. Healthy look. Eyes a little heavy this morning. How do you like that wonderful spring-water?"

"Fine. I've taken it every morning until yesterday, then I forgot."

"That was naughty. How is the appetite?"

"Splendid, till yesterday. It seemed to leave me."

"How about sleep?"

"Perfect,—till yesterday,—well, last night I had a hard struggle to go 'by-by.'"

"Foolish! That's not the way to the Land of Nod. Struggle is the road to insomnia. Relax, and wait, and don't look at your watch. Bed does you good, even if you lie awake, provided you don't worry. But tell me about the fishing. Have you enjoyed it? Was it good?"

"Excellent. I've improved a lot. Caught something every day up to yesterday. One day I landed twelve good trout, the biggest a foot long. But yesterday I got nothing."

"Yesterday! Yesterday! What the devil was wrong with yesterday? Was it an unlucky day?"

"I don't know; can't say yet. But it was certainly an amazing day, overwhelming, upsetting. Nothing like it ever happened before. It troubles me frightfully. I'll tell you about it,—in confidence."

Gilbert, evidently with some embarrassment, described the Miraculous Vision of Red Rock. He did not go into unnecessary details, but he made the outline quite clear. He was emphatic about his confusion of mind, and how much he was ashamed of himself.

Brewster concealed a smile.

"I can't see why you should be in such distress, my dear fellow, most men would consider the experience rather agreeable. It wasn't in any way your fault, was it?"

"I suppose not."

"And the girl? She was not at all to blame for it, was she?"

"By Jove, no! It's impossible to think of blame in connection with such a heavenly creature. She was so pure and perfect, I can't believe she was real."

"But she is, I can assure you; and what's more, I can tell you her name, if my guess proves right.

What was that house like? Did you notice it on your way to the pool?"

"Yes, it had a hipped roof and dormer windows, a broad piazza with white pillars, and an uncommonly big stone chimney. Cottage-colonial type, and very pretty."

"I am right, then. It was built by Adam Prime, who used to teach history to us in college. You remember him? Ten or twelve years ago his wife ran away with a play-actor, leaving Prime with a young daughter on his hands. There was some foolish gossip in the town; Prime got very angry, resigned his chair, said the town and college could go to—wherever they wanted to go—if he could only keep his child and do his work in peace. So he came up here to the Inn and built his cottage in the valley; makes his living by writing text-books and stories, amuses himself by pretending to farm. He goes into town to the Contrary Club once a month; you must have met him there. No? Not a member? Too old fogy for you, I suppose. Prime is a little odd, but a good fellow, and a most entertaining talker. Daughter's name is Evelyn,—rather pretty, isn't it—Evelyn Prime? She graduated from Smith College about a year ago; acting as secretary to her father now. She must have been your Miraculous Vision of Red Rock. But I wouldn't say anything about that at present, if I were you."

"Shouldn't I own up and behave like a man?"

"Behave like a man, by all means. You're capable of it. You're on the road to robust health. But you don't need to boast about your luck and be fresh. You must certainly go to call on the old professor to-morrow. He'll welcome you as an 'old pupil.' You'll like him, and he can tell you more about the fishing than any one in the region; he used to be a dab at it before he went lame. But listen: after lunch, (if you can give me some,) will you lend me Jenkins and your car to take me down to Stroudsburg to catch the evening express? All right. Remember, now! Be a man; hold up your head and go forward; no more silly nervous nonsense about relapses!"

IV

THE CURE

Monday was fine, and Gilbert began to feel all right again. He did not fish in the morning; in the afternoon Jenkins drove him, *sans* waders or rod, to the cottage at Red Rock. He knocked at the door, and Professor Prime opened it. He was a small gray gentleman, with a military mustache, a twinkle in his eye, and a decided limp in his left leg. He recognized his visitor almost at once.

"You look very like an old pupil of mine, Van Buren Gilbert. You are he? I am mighty glad to see you again. Come in, come in. You must tell me all about yourself, where you have been, what you have been doing. I remember I flunked you in Renascence History in Junior year; but you made it up all right, and got your sheepskin. Now sit down in this easy chair, take a pipe if you will, and give me your postgraduate report."

In the low-ceilinged room, lined with thousands of books and smelling faintly of Russian leather, the old man and the young man renewed acquaintance and built up friendship in easy talk. Prime told of his adventures in making books, some for a living and some for the pure pleasure of it; of his disappointments with the chickens and the pigs on the "farm"; of the building of the house and the trouble with smoky chimneys, which was finally conquered; of this and that and the other experience of a bookman's life in the country. Gilbert told of his brief war-service, his strenuous work in finance, his perplexing illness, and his prospect of recovery. They joined in praise of that excellent doctor, George Brewster. Then the talk fell on fishing.

"I'm afraid, sir," said Gilbert, "that I have to confess and apologize to you for an offense innocently committed. I was fishing straight down the stream one day without thinking of private rights, and I'm afraid I,—er—er, I must have trespassed on your property."

"Not at all," replied Prime heartily. "No apology is needed, for no offense has been committed. I gave my fishing rights to the Brightwater Preserve some years ago. In return I have the privilege of fishing the whole stream where and when I like. I cannot do much now, with this confounded game leg. But I can give you some points on the fishing. Now it is time for tea, which I hope you will take with us. My daughter Evelyn will serve us. She has just taken her degree at Smith College, but she is not a bluestocking. Eve! Eve!"

He called across the hall, and Eve appeared, dressed in a flowered organdie with a white fichu at the neck, quite demure. She was like a pink laurel-blossom, delicate and virginal. She carried the tea-tray; perhaps because she knew it was the sacred hour; perhaps because she preferred to have her hands occupied. She smiled and nodded gaily when Gilbert was introduced as one of the professor's old pupils.

"Ah," she said, "father finds them everywhere. They spring up around him, like flowers in the footsteps of May. I'm very glad to know you, Mr. Gilbert. You must tell me how to make your tea."

"Can a graduate of Smith College, a Maid of Arts I suppose, condescend to make tea?"

"Certainly," she replied laughing. "Don't you know that the two most popular courses at Smith are tea and theatricals? Smith girls understand acting. How do you like yours? Sugar, I guess; and then what? Milk or lemon?"

"Lemon, please," he answered, "but not too much, only a small slice. I am an invalid, and a very little acid, in books, people, or drinks, is all I can stand."

"But you don't look at all like an invalid," she said with a rapid glance at his face, "you look quite lifelike. And I understand you are an ardent angler. That doesn't sound like a sick man. Have you had much luck along our stream?"

He quickly searched her innocent-seeming eyes for a hidden meaning, and then felt sure there was none. He answered modestly.

"Some,—probably more than I deserve, for I'm only a duffer. But you know it's bad luck for an angler to brag. Let's talk about our 'bright college years.' Did I know you when your father was a professor?"

"No indeed. I was too little for a grand person like you to notice. But *I* knew *you.* You were on the football-team, weren't you? All we kidlets worshipped the team, and asked no questions about character."

"That was very lucky for me," he answered gravely.

Six o'clock came before they knew it, and the visitor said he must go, or be late for dinner at the Inn. But he promised to come back again on Wednesday when the strawberries would be ripe. So he did. Likewise on Friday, and on Sunday for an early dinner.

Thus began for Gilbert the happiest time of his life, full of contentment and comradeship and fun. There were excursions in the car to distant streams where the three picnicked joyously. Eve showed him her chickens and asked him to explain why they would persist in laying only when eggs were cheap. She had long talks with him about her favorite books and his. She took him to the top of her best-beloved hill, from which there was a glorious view over the long wooded ranges of the Alleghanies down to the sharp cuts of the Water Gap and the Wind Gap beside it. Professor Prime was a quaint and delightful companion. Gilbert no more thought of being ill again than he did of committing forgery. And Eve, —well, there are no words in the dictionary fitly to describe her.

One evening toward the end of June they had an early supper at the cottage, for the fishing was tapering off with the season, and Gilbert wanted to try the pools below Red Rock after sundown.

"I am going to tell you something special about the Brightwater fishing," said Prime. "Have you ever heard of the Silver Doctor?"

"You don't mean George Brewster, do you?"

"No, although he deserves the name. But what I mean is an artificial fly, silver body and party-colored feathers. Do you know it?"

"Yes, but I thought it was a salmon-fly."

"It is also a trout-fly, and the best on this stream, if you use it just between dusk and dark, or by early moonlight perhaps. See, here is one, tied on a number 8 hook. You must put it on your lightest leader,

—only a single fly, mind you,—and try it this evening. Fish up-stream, cast very lightly, let the fly sink an inch or two, and draw it slowly toward you. You may catch a big one."

"Father has given you the fly," said Eve, "now, Van, if you'll be very good I'll take you to the trout. I marked him down this morning, a beauty, a monster, he must weigh two pounds. He's under the rock in the deep pool. Do you know where that is?"

Did he know! Good Lord, could he ever forget! Would he ever dare to tell her how well he knew?

They went out on the edge of the dark. Eve led the way through the shadowy woods, Van followed the glimmer of her dress. At the water's brink they stopped for a moment and looked into each other's eyes by the dim moonlight. The other side of the pool was shaded.

"See," said Eve, turning away, "isn't my trout rising there at the head of the pool where the current comes in? I thought I saw a little break in the ripple. You must get that fish, he's the prize of the stream."

"I mean to get the prize of the stream to-night, if I can," said Van. He stepped very gently into the water, waded quietly up along the bank, careful to make no sound, or splash, or wave. Then he cast; once! no response; twice! the Silver Doctor lit lightly in the ripple, came slowly down and checked an instant. The angler struck with a turn of the wrist and the big fish was fast.

How he played in the moonlight and in the shade! What gallant rushes! What swift turns! Van handled him like a master. Eve watched anxiously, never giving a word of advice,—blessed girl,—but standing ready with the net when the fish came in. Van gave him the *coup de grâce* and laid him at Eve's feet. Then he washed his hands, dried them carefully on his handkerchief, and came very close to the girl.

"He's yours," he said, "but my darling Eve, woman that God made for me, I have something that I must tell you,—now,—to-night. I'm afraid, but I *must* tell you."

"What is it?" she whispered trembling.

"Nearly a month ago, coming to fish this pool I saw you bathing alone in the early morning. I didn't mean it. I couldn't help it. I prayed God to let me get away without a sound. I would rather die than make you ashamed. I love you better than all the world. Eve, can you forgive me? Won't you speak to me?"

Eve . . . asked him to explain why they would persist in laying only when eggs were cheap.

He took both her hands and drew her to him. She smiled softly and looked down.

"I did not *hear* you," she whispered, "but I *saw* you for an instant. I was ashamed *then*,—a little,— but not *now*,—since we love each other."

She lifted her face to him, and they kissed full on the lips.

"THE HEAD THAT WEARS
A CROWN"

"THE HEAD THAT WEARS
A CROWN"

THE head of Mirande Amélie, reigning sovereign of the Principality of Wallenburg, was most lovely to look at. Masses of dark-brown hair above a forehead pure and smooth as alabaster; eyes of deep blue almost violet in certain lights; nostrils fine and sensitive, over a rosy mouth that was at once proud and gentle; the upper lip rather short, the lower a little full, a wistful mouth; chin delicately firm and rounded, completing the clean oval of the warm pale face; this perfection of maiden beauty at twenty years was carried on a slim white neck rising from a body tall and slender, supple and strong. It was like a wild rose. It was like a virgin lily. God knows what it was like, for he never made anything else so singularly beautiful and appealing.

That was what Herbert Dabney, (American engineer and youngest vice-president of the Nazareth Steel Company,) thought when he was presented to the Princess in private audience by the dry old diplomat who represented the United States at the Court

of Wallenburg, as well as in the neighboring Kingdom of Neerlandia. His Excellency Pierre Eyden, the
aged Minister of State, who had nursed the little Principality like a baby for nearly thirty years and who
loved Mirande Amélie like a favorite grandchild,
stood at one side of his adored Mistress, the American
Minister at the other. An image of immortal youth
between two statues of enduring age. Dabney's
heart was still capable of quick and strong emotions of admiration and devotion. He felt them
now, as he made his formal salutation and waited,
according to etiquette, for this royal girl to address
the first question to him.

She bade him welcome graciously and asked what
errand brought him to Wallenburg at this time.

"Madam," he answered, "the Nazareth Steel
Company has sent me to study, if your Royal Highness will permit, some of the methods of steel-
making used in your dominion."

"But," she replied in a soft voice, speaking excellent English with an accent delicate as the fragrance
of a pansy, "I thought that you Americans were already the greatest steel-makers in the world. What
can you learn from a little country like mine?"

"Madam," said Dabney, "your Royal Highness

knows that it is not size which determines the ability to teach. There is an electrical process in use here in making steel of which I have heard much and should like to learn more, with your consent."

"An inquiring spirit is always to be encouraged," she said, with a slight smile, "at least when it inquires with a friendly purpose like yours. You know I have many of my people now living in the United States, not less than two hundred and fifty thousand, just about as many as there are here in Wallenburg. Can you tell me if they do well? Are they good citizens, as our friend the American Minister here assures me that they are?"

"Excellent, madam," said Dabney. "So far as my knowledge goes the Wallenburgers are one of the best elements in our foreign-born population; industrious, self-reliant, orderly, they make fine citizens. We should be glad to have more of them."

"Ah, no," she answered, shaking her head, "we have too few at home. Yet perhaps they would be better off in your country, *now*." (A sadness passed over her face, like rain over a summer landscape.) "Now that Wallenburg has been invaded and occupied,—not conquered, you understand,—it is hard for my people to earn a living. They suffer. I suffer with them, for I am their Princess." (A ray of proud sunlight broke through the rain-cloud.) "Your visit to the steel-mills will be arranged, Mr. Dabney, by my Minister of State. And we shall wish you to dine with us at our Summer Castle soon."

As Dabney made his parting bows he looked to see if there was a crown on the young monarch's head. He saw only a circlet of rich pearls, glistening on her brown hair like celestial tears.

The three men went down the long stone steps of the ancient Spanish palace into the narrow streets of Wallenburg. The American Minister's automobile was waiting, for he had to hasten back to his principal post in the famous capital of Neerlandia, a city dedicated to world-peace in the midst of world-war. As he stepped into the car he shook hands warmly with Pierre Eyden, for whom he had a deep affection and respect.

"*Au revoir*, Excellency. Please take good care of our young friend here, and keep an eye on him. He is younger than he looks. I'm afraid he is a rather romantic man of business."

"That is sometimes the best kind," said Eyden, with his genial smile. "But don't worry, my dear colleague. I'll keep an eye on him like an old motherly eagle. I'm taking him home to luncheon with me now. You must come to see us again as soon as you can. My royal mistress likes Americans, and you are *persona grata*."

Eyden's home was a modest, ancient house between the Ministry of Foreign Affairs and the Cathedral with its twisted columns. The ceilings were low, the rooms small, the furniture well worn; but an air of dignity and ease pervaded the house, rare pictures and mementos hung on the walls, the capacious cellars were stocked with precious vintages of the Saar, the Moselle, and the Marne valleys, and the golden hillsides of Burgundy. Here in a contented bachelorhood Pierre Eyden lived in his eightieth year, cared for by his faithful old servants, and still unwearied in his devotion to his chosen task of preserving the independence of his small country and watching over his beloved Princess.

He was a statesman of extraordinary ability and insight, a singularly accomplished man of the world, who had been on familiar friendly terms with both Bismarck and Thiers. In fact you might almost call him a genius living by choice in a narrow sphere. First, last, and all the time his life was for Wallenburg. If you had opened his heart you would have found written inside of it *Mirande Amélie*. Naturally it was about his sovereign that he began the intimate conversation with Dabney when the coffee and cigars were brought in after luncheon.

"What did you think of our Princess of Wallenburg?"

"Excellency," said Dabney, a little embarrassed, "I cannot tell you because I have no words fine enough. Certainly she is the most gracious and exquisite royalty I have ever dreamed of."

Eyden nodded his gray head, and his brown eyes, set in his brown face above his white beard, glowed approval.

"Yes, she is all that, and more! She is a good girl, *une très bonne fille*, one of the best and purest hearts that ever lived. That is why, loving her as I have done since her childhood, I am terribly sorry for her. She is going through purgatory,—she who does not need it! Her God, in whom she believes absolutely, ought to have spared her that."

"But, sir," stammered Dabney, somewhat amazed and bewildered by the old man's impassioned frankness, "I am afraid I don't understand you. You must make allowance for my ignorance. I come from the other side of the Atlantic where we know little about the minor affairs of Europe, except as our trade touches them. If it is not indiscreet, I would beg you to explain to me why and how your lovely Princess suffers so much?"

"'Minor affairs' is good," grunted Eyden, "you Americans measure things only on the large scale! I should like you to know that in principle this case of Wallenburg is one of the major affairs." (Then his face softened and he spoke more genially.) "But I am sure that you are an honorable young man, and if you can bear with a long talk from a veteran, I will 'put you wise'—isn't that your New York phrase?—to the situation of our little country and its sovereign."

"Nothing could please me better," said Dabney, earnestly. "You need not fear that what you choose to say will be repeated. Some of us Americans know the old rules of hospitality. You have no 'rose' hanging from your ceiling. But I take it conversation around the dining-table is always *sub rosa* and confidential."

"Good," said Eyden, "I can trust you. Take a fresh cigar and prepare to listen. You know what Wallenburg is, a table-land of a thousand square miles, lifted up in the midst of great jealous nations.

Half of it is rough and cold, the other half is smooth and warm, but all of it is beautiful and rich, either in fertile fields, abundant forests, or productive mines. Consequently for centuries the big kingdoms quarrelled over it and grabbed it one from the other, like a football. But all the time the Wallenburgers wanted nothing but peace and liberty."

"Modest wishes," said Dabney, "but hard to obtain in Europe in those days."

"Yes, and hard now, God knows. But they were granted to Wallenburg in the first half of the nineteenth century. It was made an independent state with a parliament, but under a crown-union with Neerlandia, so that the King of that country was also Prince of Wallenburg. It kept the peace, but it didn't work well. Wallenburg suffered and the people were discontented.

"Then a very curious thing came up. Wallenburg had the Salic Law which forbids a woman to occupy the throne. But when the old King of Neerlandia died in 1890, after the death of his two good-for-little sons, it was clear that his kingdom must pass to his young daughter. Equally clear that the constitution of Wallenburg would prevent her from wearing the crown of our country. What to do?

"The crown-union was dissolved by mutual consent. According to a family compact another branch of the same House was called to our throne. Then the most curious thing happened. Our first Prince was a fine man but already old. He died leaving only one son. This son, our second Prince, had an excellent wife who bore him six children, *all girls*. Then he fell into what was plainly a fatal illness. No male heir!

"The situation was embarrassing, almost absurd. Again, what to do? Simple answer: set aside the Salic Law. So we did. After her father's death, in 1912, the eldest and finest of the six fair sisters succeeded him on the throne and a woman wore the crown of Wallenburg. Wasn't that passing strange?"

"It was indeed," said Dabney, "most extraordinary! Almost like *Kismet.*"

"Perhaps so," said Eyden, "I know little about those celestial matters. But it was not a happy fate for my dear Princess. She has a fine mind, a noble spirit. But her nature is sensitive, tender, extremely devout. She takes religion very seriously. As a girl she did not want to be a Queen; her desire was to follow the religious life, to devote herself to good works. She used to say that her sister Gertrude,—a bolder, more adventurous nature, called in childhood 'that little imp Gertrude,'—ought to have been born before her. Her mother and I had a hard time in persuading Princess Mirande Amélie that it was her Christian duty to accept the place God gave her and do her good works there. All the Wallenburgers loved her. To change the order of succession would be dangerous, might lead to conflicts and upset the whole situation. At last she yielded and took the crown she did not want."

"Such a crown," said Dabney, "must be heavy for a head so young and fair."

"Heavy!" cried the old Minister. "It is crushing. For look what has happened now! The great Powers absolutely neutralized our land in 1867; razed our only fortress; reduced our army to two hundred and fifty men; positively forbade us to have anything to do with war. That was exactly what we wanted: peace and prosperity and to mind our own business. We got it for a little while. But now the greatest of the powers that made Wallenburg neutral and disarmed her has violated the neutrality which it created and swore to protect!

"Listen! That low thunder which you can hear all the time, and which sometimes shakes the windows, is the roar of battle in Gallia, forty miles south of us. It has been roaring that way more than a year. Thousands of guns, a million soldiers, were sent through *neutral* Wallenburg by our big Eastern neighbor to make that battle. It was a breach of the law of nations, an act of dishonor, a damnable outrage! But what could we do? Nothing but protest. We had been disarmed.

"The little motor-car of the Princess, drawn up across the road where thousands of soldiers were pouring in unasked, could not stop them. They shoved it into the ditch. She wept. They laughed and sang their raucous songs,—and made their army headquarters in her city.

"They say they are not at war with Wallenburg, have not attacked or annexed our land, only *occupied* it to protect the railways against Gallia. But Gallia was our good friend and never violated our neutrality. Occupied? They have *enslaved* our land. Ten thousand soldiers here as a garrison! Everything regulated, restricted, ticketed. You must have twelve bread and meat cards to buy food. A ham costs fifty dollars. The glove-makers and glass-blowers have no work. The poor are starving, in rags. The Princess weeps every day with her suffering people, but she can do nothing. There are intrigues, plots, divisions in the Court. Some idiots urge her to marry a Teuton princelet or dukeling. *Pfui!* That would be accepting insult with injury. She would rather die. Don't you see now why I grieve for her?"

"I see, sir," answered Dabney, his deep voice deepening, his clean-cut bronzed face glowing, "and I tell you, Excellency, though I have only seen your Princess once, I think a man would gladly encounter death to spare that lady any pain or shame."

The old Statesman looked at him keenly under shaggy eyebrows.

"So?" he said. "I knew you were rich, and handsome, and a power in the business world. Now I perceive also that you are one of those highly chivalrous Southerners of whom I have read in novels."

"At your service, sir,—Herbert Dabney of Eastover Hall, Virginia!"

"Well, well; pray do not take offense where none was intended. Youth is splendid but sometimes inconsiderate. I hope you will not indulge any romantic dreams after the charming but impossible style of *The Prisoner of Zenda.*"

"Don't worry, sir," said Dabney. "I confess to

being an enthusiast, but not an ass. I know what is due to a crowned head. But is there any reason why your Princess should not have the admiring loyalty of a young man as well as the life-long devotion of an old man?"

"Very well put," said Eyden, nodding. "I feel sure you are to be trusted. You shall have as much opportunity of seeing the Princess as possible in the present disturbed condition of court and social affairs. Her Royal Highness has instructed me to give you a permit to visit all the steel-works, and to put two men of her little police-army at your disposal as an escort for your car. You will not really need them. You see you came to us well recommended in advance; and friendly connections with the United States will be valuable to us for many reasons. If you stay here a month or two, as I believe you propose, you will need outdoor exercise. The two worthwhile sports of Wallenburg are reh-shooting in the forests, which is fair, and trout-fishing in the little rivers, which is excellent at this season. You shall have a permit for both, including the royal estates which are considerable. I regret to have a meeting of the Council in half an hour. Come to see me soon again, and let me know of anything that you want."

II

Dabney dined alone that night in the high vaulted dining-room of the Hotel Bossert; smoked pipe after pipe of Virginia tobacco on the iron balcony of his comfortable rooms; grimly watched two field-gray squads of the garrison marching glum and sullen to their posts on the railway; listened to the sound like distant thunder muttering of the madness of mankind under a pure night of dripping stars; and then went to bed, falling easily into a valley of sleep.

Beautiful dreams walked gently through his slumber. Tall slender dreams, clothed in violet, pearl-crowned, with sorrowful kind eyes and wistful lips. They did not break his perfect rest. They were sad, but they brought with them a strange feeling of comfort, almost happiness. From the sweetest and most moving of these visions of the night he woke to sunlight pouring in at his windows and a joyful sense of the day's work before him.

Colonel Marrtes, commandant of the foreign garrison, had politely called and left his card. This pasteboard courtesy reciprocated in proper form, Dabney motored south to visit the iron-furnaces and steel-mills in that district. The business that he did there

does not concern this story. It was successful as far
as it went. He made some pleasant acquaintances:
John Davison, a young engineer from Cornell who
had been working in the establishment at Asch for
five years and who has a part in this story later:
Adolf Mersch, the big, forceful head of the steel
concern, the man who kept things going no matter
what happened. Quite deaf, happy, genial, full of
shrewdness for his competitors and kindness for his
thousands of work-people, Mersch was also a confirmed angler. When he heard that Dabney was
given to the same harmless lunacy he insisted that
his visitor must go with him next day on a fishing-
party to his own little river in the north, the Carfe.

Happy day! Three charming merry ladies in the
party, with Mersch and Davison and Dabney; lunch
spread on the greensward beside an old white inn;
soft sunlight over the steep folding hills and the long
curving valley; a stream that flowed with clear and
silent speed between flowery meadows and deepened
into pools where the big trout rose eagerly to the fly.
An Izaak Walton day! But light airs from the south
breathing up the valley brought faintly that ominous
muttering as of distant thunder to Dabney's ears.
Before him, as he fished alone up-stream, walked ever

that slender dream in violet with pearls, and he was companied by "the star-like sorrows of immortal eyes."

Two more days he spent in visiting the mines and forges of the mountainous west of the principality and making acquaintances there and in the city. On the third day he went out by himself to try the Ellert, a wildish waterfally stream marking the western border of the extensive domain of the Summer Castle. In places the little river almost filled a narrow gorge between carved and broken cliffs twenty or thirty feet high. As he passed through one of these places, deep-bowered in massive beech-trees and spreading firs, he heard voices above him, chattering, singing, laughing, calling out. Then a voice that his heart knew cried in sharp terror, "Come back! you will fall!"

He looked up and saw on the edge of the cliff a little group of women and children in white walking-dress. A weathered crag of limestone like a pillar jutted out from the cliff, joined to it only by a narrow ridge of crumbly rock. On top of this pinnacle stood a child of perhaps eight years, long hair loose on her shoulder, arms outstretched, shouting "Look at me! I am the Nixie of the stream. I can't fall!"

But already her voice trembled; her eyes had fear in them. Her footing was so narrow that she could not turn; a touch, a sudden noise, perhaps even a downward look, would topple her down to death or maiming. What to do?

A pace beyond the pillar and perhaps ten feet lower was a smoother sloping ledge of rock, moss-covered. Here the man climbed noiselessly. Holding out his arms he quietly commanded the child.

"Fly down, Nixie. I am the Lord of the Stream. I will catch you."

Something in the tone of the deep voice, the look of the strong kind face, mastered the pranksome creature. She jumped boldly and his arms clasped her.

"Naughty Nixie," he laughed. But she put her hands on his shoulders and pushed herself back.

"Remember your manners," she said. "I am *Altesse*, Highness!"

"Highness," he answered with mocking gravity, "let me bring you a little higher,—up to your royal sister."

She nestled on his shoulder. He carried her carefully up the steep bank and set her down in front of the Princess.

"How can we thank you, sir?" she said, holding

out her hand, trembling slightly. "You arrived in the nick of time. You have rendered us a very great service."

He touched the hand, bowing over it; then with a frank look into her face he said, "Madam, if the service to you were far greater I should be the more glad, and ask no thanks."

Her cheeks showed a mounting color as she answered slowly: "But you must accept them, all the same. Now I will present you to the woodland company in our favorite playground. Mr. Dabney of Virginia; my sisters, Gertrude, Antonia, Marta, Ottilie, and Irma, the wildest of us after Gertrude; my junior lady-in-waiting and dear companion, Countess Montjoie; and look, coming over the hill there are our supposed guardians, my chamberlain Baron Peyrouse and the commander of my toy army Major Van Doorn, rather late for their duty. You will meet all these people when you dine with us day after to-morrow. But our meeting to-day must be forgotten, otherwise little Irma will be scolded by her mother and punished. That I do not wish. Can you forget, monsieur?"

"Princess, I cannot forget easily, but I can keep silence splendidly."

"That is a specially good quality for a knight errant of damsels in distress. Till Thursday evening, then, *au revoir*."

The dinner was an informal family affair, though richly served with fine food and rare wines. Dabney was duly presented to the Dowager Princess, a stately pale lady in deep black; then to the five princesses, who suppressed their giggles, with twinkling, curious eyes; then to the two ladies-in-waiting, (did the rosy Countess Montjoie nearly wink at him?); then to the stout chamberlain and the thin, earnest-looking Major Van Doorn, troubled by the responsibility of his toy army in a situation which might at any hour become perilous for his Mistress. Minister Eyden did the presenting gravely but with a funny look, as if he knew a good joke that he could not tell.

The conversation was general, carefully avoiding European politics, but rambling over America, its magical new cities, its wonderful mountains and rivers, its vast plains, once barren, now swiftly enchanted by water into fertility. Dabney could answer questions about these things more readily than most Americans, who boast of the bigness of their country, but seem to love it so little that they do not care to visit it. His professional work as well as his keen passion for sport had led him into every State of the Union.

"I think," said he, "that we have two real cities, New York and San Francisco. Some of the others are wealthy, active, magnificent, like enormous villages suddenly grown rich and powerful. Even Washington, beautiful as it is in spots, is little more than a luxurious camp for politicians and diplomats and a fine location for memorials. My friends in Chicago, or Philadelphia, or St. Louis, or Los Angeles, would annihilate me for saying this. The old Bostonians would scalp me with cold contempt. But it seems to me true."

"The rest of the world," said the Princess, at whose left he was sitting, "has an idea that Americans worship only bigness and wealth."

"Not all of us, and not altogether," he answered quietly. "There are other things for which we care more. Beauty, strength of heart, order with freedom, fine ideals with simple manners."

"But we hear that you spoil your women," she said smiling, "you indulge them too much."

"Impossible, madam," he replied. "It is right to indulge a fine woman, but she cannot be spoiled."

Then the talk turned on sport. He told modestly of hunting bighorn sheep in Montana, mountain-lions in Utah, and Kadiak bears in Alaska. Gertrude and one of her sisters expressed an interest in fly-fishing and a wish to learn the gentle art. Dabney said he would gladly teach them what he knew, if it was permitted.

The ladies rose, following the Princess. The gentlemen did not linger long over their cigars and coffee. Led by the stout chamberlain they rejoined the ladies in the great drawing-room. The Princess told Dabney that she wished him to see her garden of fox-glove and delphinium in the moonlight. They looked out upon it from the bay window at the far end of the room. Serene and delicate, the flowers lifted their heads in the cool radiance as if to meet the embrace of Diana.

"Isn't it entrancing?" said the girl, "so beautiful that it brings sad thoughts to my mind." Then with a sudden turn she continued. "Mr. Dabney, I should like to hear more about your country, I mean about the hills and valleys, the quiet places. It would rest me. Perhaps also I should like to tell you more about my own country. It would be a relief to speak to such a listener. Often in the afternoons I walk

with Montjoie along the woodland path above the
Ellert. If you should be fishing on the stream and
see me on the path and climb up, it would be no in-
trusion."

"Princess," he said, "you are most gracious to me.
I shall not fail."

Three days later, idling attentively down the
Ellert, he looked up through green branches and
caught a glimpse of a white dress at the top of the
cliff. He climbed and found the Princess on a rustic
bench under an old beech-tree with a book open on
her knees. He made his bow, smilingly declined the
place she offered him on the bench, and sat on the
grass at her feet, looking up to her.

They talked of hills and valleys, of forests and
streams, of the friendly silent trees that are a refuge
from noisy people, of the sweet natural things, yes,
and the great elemental powers, the stars, the wide
waters, the winds, that speak of God. Then she
talked of her loved Wallenburg, of its present op-
pression and misery, of her own perplexity in the
midst of intrigues, her shame at being forced into
even an indirect connection with a war after the great
nations had sworn that her country should always
be neutral and at peace.

"Many a night I cannot sleep for the pain of it. Many a day my soul is harrowed by the suffering of my people. Those poor glove-makers! Only a quarter of them have work now. They take it by turns. Those that work divide their earnings with those that are forced to be idle. You know I did not want the crown. But when my mother and my dear Minister Eyden persuaded me that it was my duty to accept it, I told my people in plain words what it was that I desired. To be a good sovereign; to interest myself in all; to be fair, easy of access, ready to give aid; to try to realize within our small limits the Beautiful, the True, the Good; above all to keep the honor and independence of my country intact by observing the neutrality to which we were pledged. That was what I said. That was what I swore to do. And now,—dear God, look at it, have pity!"

The tears overflowed and rolled down her face. Dabney was shaken to the core. Yet his voice was clear and steady when he spoke.

"Princess, I understand. My whole heart feels for you. If there were anything in the world I could do for you, I would thank God."

"But there is nothing,—except to comprehend and sympathize."

"If that is any help it is altogether yours. One thing more." (He hesitated an instant, then restrained himself firmly and went on.) "I want you to know my belief that you have done more to preserve your country from riot and rapine than any man could have done. Your patience has been an example. Your fortitude in trial, your wise and calm words of counsel have kept your people from a hopeless revolt. You have saved Wallenburg from the worst."

"Ah, that is good hearing, my friend. You have helped me much. We must talk again. Montjoie will be looking for me now. For to-day, farewell!"

He kissed the hand that she held out to him, and went down into the valley. The tall slender dream moved before him up the stream, through the green shade. It was not clothed now in violet and pearls, but in pure white.

Twice more, at longer intervals, these two had comradeship under the beech-tree and exchanged— what? Not declarations of passion and mutual embraces. But something more rare and sacred,— more heavenly.

The last time he came to say good-bye. He must

go home to America, to do his duty, part of which was to help his country to see that she must enter the war to end it and deliver the world from its horror and anguish. Because it was the last time, he spoke more freely and openly of what they both knew so well.

She had been talking of the varied natural beauty of America. She asked which of its valleys he thought most beautiful.

"The fairest of our valleys," he answered, "to my mind, is the Shenandoah, my home country. I wish that you could see it. Would God I could bring you there into happy peace. I would carry you on my hands, give you all your heart desires, serve you with my whole life. You know already that I love you far above all women."

"Yes," she said, looking at him tenderly, "surely I know. It makes me glad and proud and sad, for you are most dear to me." (She laid her thin hand on her breast as if to check something that fluttered there. Then she continued, laying the same white hand upon his brown one.) "You know as well as I do that it is impossible. This grief we must share. If—if—we had met five years ago,—who knows? But we have to do now not with ifs,—but with things as they are. I must,—what is that old Scotch word, —I must 'dree my weird,' carry my heavy crown. Then if God brings my country free and safe I am vowed to Him who bore a crown of thorns for all of us. Do you understand?"

"Perfectly. I shall remember what I owe you as long as I live. Most dear Princess, in three days I shall be gone. God bless and keep you forever."

Stooping to kiss the hand that lay on his he felt it lifted to his lips, pressed closely against his mouth. He walked down into the forest like a blind man, led by the hand of his white dream.

III

But it was more than three days before Herbert Dabney set out for home. This is how it happened.

On the second evening before the appointed day of departure he was in the Café "Star of Wallen-burg" with his friends Davison and Pellatori, a gentleman of Italian blood whose family had been settled for two generations in Wallenburg and had made splendid benefactions to the city. He was married to a Belgian countess, and they lived in a charming hunting-lodge some three miles out of town on

the edge of a deer-forest. The things said in that
house about the Imperial army of "occupation"
could not be repeated outside.

There were thirty or forty people in the café,
mostly Wallenburgers, quietly drinking their beer, or
playing dominos, or talking of harmless affairs. But
at a small table where three men were sitting not far
from Dabney there was more noise. Two of them
were horse-dealers who had suddenly grown rich.
The third was a Borussian named Quieregg,—Von
Quieregg he called himself,—a loud-tongued, scar-
cheeked, pimply fellow with bulbous eyes. He had
been cashiered from the army for conduct unbecoming an officer and a gentleman. But owing to his
skill in languages a use had been found for him in the
lowest branch of the secret service as an *agent provo-
cateur*. He was holding forth to his companions and
anybody else that chose to hear, in that booming,
trampling voice in which men of his type betray
themselves when excited.

"America!" he said, "what is America? A big
mushroom. A puff-ball. An ignorant nation of ped-
dlers and bluffers. America will do anything for
money and nothing without. She is cowardly and
greedy. She will never enter the war until she gets

her price. Who will pay it? She is a strumpet for sale to the highest bidder."

Dabney's brows were black and his clinched jaws grew white. He would have risen, but his friends held him back. The Wallenburgers eyed him with curiosity and sympathy. The infatuated Quieregg boomed on.

"There are women like that even among the highborn. This little mealy-mouthed Princess here— what is she? A trickster in a country of doubledealers. She plays false, false with both sides. She professes that her honor is offended, but she tries even now to entrap one of our fine Borussian princes——"

An angry murmur ran through the room. Chairs grated and fell as they were pushed back. Men sprang to their feet. There was a buzzing like a swarm of furious bees.

Dabney shook off his friends' hands, and rose quickly. He had the ominous look, frowning eyes and twisted smiling mouth, well known of old on the faces of "the duelling Dabneys of Eastover."

"Please let me pass, gentlemen," he said to the others. "My country has been insulted. This is my affair."

He stepped quietly over to Quieregg's table, carrying a full glass of wine without spilling a drop. He rested the fingers of one hand on the table, leaning slightly forward and holding the wine-glass in the other.

"*Dummer Junge*," he said, (for he had been in a student corps at Heidelberg and knew the fighting words,) "*Schweinhund*, you have dared to speak ill of my country. You are a lost liar. You have defamed *her*, the pure and noble. You have spit your venom at *her*, the highest of all. Your mouth is foul. Wash it with this!"

He threw the wine into the pale pimply face. Then he spoke in a very low voice inaudible to the room at large.

"My friend, Mr. Davison, will be at the Hotel Bossert this evening. No doubt you will send one of your friends to arrange the cartel."

He walked with Pellatori and Davison through the narrow streets to his hotel.

To Davison he said: "Let the cartel be simple. The choice will be ours. Pistols; sunrise to-morrow; twelve paces; one shot. I will smash that lying mouth forever."

To Pellatori he said: "I ask your help, sir. Have

you a pair of matched pistols? Do you know of a quiet place? Can this be arranged without scandal?"

"Yes, to all three questions," replied Pellatori. "But the last is the most difficult. I have a pair of pistols, of the finest Italian make. I shall bring them within the hour to Mr. Davison, so that both parties can examine them. As to the place, there is an open glade in the forest back of my house,—you know where that is,—no one ever passes there in the early morning. As to scandal, it will be difficult, but I think it can be prevented. I am not an ardent admirer of the Princess, yet there is no reason why a lady's name should be dragged into this. Your country was grossly insulted in your presence,—intolerable to a man of honor. *She* whom you adore was publicly defamed by that dirty, arrogant sculpin. You are a high-spirited, sensitive man,—a man after my own heart. Frankly, I do not see how you could have acted otherwise than you did. I have some influence with the newspapers here and shall use it to choke gossip. We shall not meet to-morrow, but I shall wish you well. A sound sleep will help you. Good night."

"I shall have it. Six hours at least. I thank you

heartily, Signor Pellatori, and bid you adieu,—and
au plaisir."

The cartel was satisfactorily arranged between
Davison and one of Quieregg's horse-dealers. The
morning sun rose fair above the oval glade; shining
dew on the short grass; small birds singing merrily
on the sunny westward side; on the eastward side the
shadow lingered, but the light was beautifully clear.

The principals were placed here by their seconds,
at twelve paces. A surgeon from the hospital, confidential friend of Pellatori, had opened his instrument
case under the trees. The word was given: one—
two—three—a split second before the last word was
completed the Borussian fired.

The ball struck the Virginian's right forearm,
breaking the smaller bone. He caught the loaded
pistol in his left hand, took a gray-squirrel aim, and
hit his adversary on the side of the chin. The bullet
shattered the right jaw-bone and glanced on into the
woods. It was a ghastly wound, but not necessarily
fatal.

The surgeon did the emergency bandaging for
both men, with despatch. Two motor-cars were
waiting on the border of the wood. Quieregg was
hurried to the hospital, where he disappears from

the story. Dabney, in much pain but able to sit up and to walk, found himself at the door of Eyden's time-worn house. As if he had been expected he was quietly installed in the guest-chamber, where the gray-haired butler had already arranged his luggage.

"I told them at the hotel, sir, that when you came in from hunting you were going to stay with His Excellency a few days. Was that right, sir?"

"It was," said Dabney, grinning in spite of his pain, "quite right! Now help me out of my clothes, but very carefully, please. I hurt my arm in the forest. I want to lie down awhile."

At noon, when the doctor had finished sterilizing the wound, setting the bone, binding the splints, Dabney looked up into the quizzical face of Pierre Eyden at the foot of his bed.

"My young friend, you once told me that you were an enthusiast, but *not an ass*. I think you were mistaken."

"Perhaps I was."

"Not perhaps, but certainly! Rather a lovable ass, however. It is the people we love who often make us the most trouble."

"Honestly, I'm sorry."

"And honestly, I'm not so sorry as I'm busy. You

know Wallenburg is a small place, full of spies. Rumors in a small place run around like—like cockroaches in an old kitchen. The first thing we have to do is to give the right news a good start. This is what will be in the papers this afternoon and to-morrow morning."

Dabney took the proof-slip in his hand and read the paragraph in the local language.

REGRETTABLE ACCIDENT

Herr von Quieregg, a stranger within our gates but quite well known in Wallenburg, has suffered a severe and dangerous accident. The Herr is devoted to the chase, and as he was hunting in the forest south of the city, just at sunrise, he made a misstep and fell. The gun was discharged and the ball struck him in the mouth, inflicting a grave but not necessarily fatal wound. He is now in the Pellatori Hospital, receiving the best of care and nursing. It is hoped that he will ultimately recover. But his powers of speech, which were somewhat unusual, may be permanently impaired.

"Will the people be satisfied with that?" asked Dabney, grinning.

"Entirely," answered Eyden, grinning back, "the people will be highly satisfied when they read that news about a dirty spy."

"But will they believe it is the whole story?"

337

"The *people* will. As a matter of fact every word of it is true. They will not ask what he was hunting, or what kind of a misstep he made, or whose gun was discharged. But the *inner circle*, those who really want to know things, will certainly ask for more information."

"What will they be told?"

"Privately, that a hot-headed young Virginian, hearing his country traduced and vilified in a public place by a stranger, took it as an unforgivable insult, demanded satisfaction,—and got it."

"Will that be all?"

"Yes, that will be all, for the inner circle. The *inmost circle*,—tried and faithful ones, half a dozen of us,—will know without telling that there was really something more, but they will never give a name to it. That exalted name must not be touched by gossip. Understand, young man, you have been rash and careless about that name."

"My God, sir, no! I would die to defend it."

"That is precisely what you must not do. You must live and keep your mouth shut.

"Now listen, this is about yourself. Colonel Marrtes called on me this morning. He regards you as a suspicious person, dangerous to the peace of

Wallenburg. He says your presence here can be tolerated no longer. You must be told to go home at once or run the risk of being arrested, imprisoned, perhaps shot as a spy. Curse his arrogance! But he has the power. I gave my word that you should be practically interned in my house and sent home as soon as you recovered from your accident,—a broken arm. He laughed, and said that would be correct. Marrtes is quite a decent fellow in some ways, spite of his arrogance. The doctor says you will probably be able to travel in four days. We shall put you in your car with one of our own soldiers in uniform beside your chauffeur. You can take the same road you used coming in. I shall go with you to our frontier. From Neerlandia your excellent Minister, (my best regards to him,) can easily secure a homeward passage for you. Is that all right?"

"Perfectly. I thank you warmly for everything. Now, if you will excuse me, I should like to sleep."

The broken arm behaved well. There was no fever. In the late afternoon of the third day Eyden came in, his face a mask of his thought.

"There is a nun down-stairs,—a Poor Clare,— looks like a nursing sister. She wants to see you. May she come up?"

"What do you think about it?"

"She says she has a message for you,—for your ear alone. Shall I let her come?"

"By all means!"

The Poor Clare entered the room and stood quietly by the bed, looking down at him with sisterly compassion. There was something familiar to him in the slender form wearing the dark robe. Under the stiff white coif concealing hair and brow, the eyes of violet-blue were not the eyes of a stranger. When she spoke her low voice thrilled him with remembrance.

"I come at the wish of a lady who knows you, and wishes you well. She has heard of your accident. She thinks you have done wrong. But she is not angry with you,—oh, no! She wants to hear of your health."

"It is better every minute,—every second."

"As for me,—I am only the poor Sister Miranda, —I think you could not help doing what you did. I honor you for it. God will forgive you. I will remember it and pray for you at His altar. See, here is that lady's picture with her name written. But you must not open it now."

"With all my heart I thank you, Sister Miranda, —and that lady! Can I send her a message?"

"Easily."

"Let her know, then, how much better I am,—far better since you came,—and everlastingly grateful. Tell her I shall be fighting soon in a finer way,— fighting against war,—fighting for her deliverance and the liberty of her country. Let her know surely that I shall never forget and always be glad."

"She will surely know."

"And now, kind Sister,—dear Sister *Mirande Amélie*,—would it be right for you to complete your ministry of healing by giving me a parting kiss?"

"It would be right. Not one, but three."

Her lips lightly touched each of his closed eyes. Then his mouth, which answered.

"For silence and faithful memory," she whispered.

He opened his eyes. She was passing through the doorway with bowed head. He never saw her again.

IV

When Herbert Dabney reached New York his first duty was to make his confidential report to the Nazareth directors about the steel business in Wallenburg. Owing to the disturbed condition of Europe nothing definite and practical could be done at present. But there was certain valuable information to be conveyed, there were certain tentative plans and "gentlemen's agreements" in regard to patents, royalties, divisions of the field, and so on,—to be considered when the orgy of bloodshed and destruction was ended. The report was satisfactory and promising as far as possible. Dabney, having been duly thanked and congratulated, resigned his vice-presidency, joined the officers' training-camp at Plattsburg, and after his course there began to make speeches before learned and patriotic societies throughout the country. Some of the things he said were remembered.

"As long as secret treaties are kept through fear and open treaties violated by force the world will not be safe for any kind of peaceful government."

"America's bigness protects her, for the present, from every enemy except selfishness, cowardice, and greed."

"Peace without victory is splendid, but sometimes victory is the only road to peace."

"If our forefathers had received half the outrage that has been thrust upon our lawful trade and travel, they would have taken arms to end it two years ago."

"The vital interests of these United States are now world-wide. Our duties as a Great Power cover the same latitude and longitude."

"Certainly we should mind our own business. But we can't mind it unless we keep it."

"Isolation is a peril if it means insulation. To have no foes is a happy state. But it is too costly to buy at the price of having no friends."

When at last America was forced to enter the war, Dabney was one of the first to volunteer and be commissioned. He fought in the Argonne, was decorated, wounded in the same old arm, and sent to the great hospital at Neuilly. After the Armistice, being convalescent, he tried to get a three days' leave and a permit to visit Wallenburg. For some unknown reason it was denied him. "Regret—impossible at present."

All he could learn of the Principality was that his friend Pierre Eyden had died of age and trouble. There had been political controversies and conflicts, almost a riot in the street before the old Spanish Palace. The Princess had come out on the balcony and spoken the people calm. Soon after, she had resigned the crown in favor of her sister, and intended to enter a Bavarian convent where a relative of hers was Abbess.

This was all the news. It moved Dabney deeply. He could not tell whether regret or relief was the dominant feeling. He wrote a letter which was never answered, perhaps because it was not delivered. The mail of abdicating royalties is not very secure or regular.

Then he went to the United States to get his honorable discharge from the service. The business world had no more attraction for him. He had wealth enough and no worldly ambition to gratify. All that he wanted was a man's life in quiet with a chance to do a little good.

Eastover Hall in the Shenandoah Valley, among his "own people," with its white-pillared portico looking down the long avenue of trees that his grandfather had planted and over the broad acres of tilth and woodland where he had rambled as a boy, called him irresistibly home.

He raised fine cattle, and "farmed it" with his one good arm. He looked after the welfare of his workpeople, building new houses for them, new schools for the colored children, and co-operating with his neighbors to erect and endow a modern hospital in the near-by village. He fished for bass in the summer, hunted partridges in the fall, rode to hounds in the winter.

In all these comings and goings, honest tasks and simple pleasures, he was companioned by his ineffable dream. He saw her now in violet and pearls, smiling at him; again, in pure white, reading under a smooth beech-tree; again, in the long robe of a nun, with her dark blue eyes glowing under her snowy coif and her red lips bending over him for a sister's farewell. Always the vision brought him sorrow and comfort and inspiration. He was content. He had known the best in the world. She stayed with him in his soul, in his good work.

One night as he sat before the open wood fire, reading by the clear light of four tall candles,—the light he preferred to all others because it was most pure and soft,—a foreign letter was brought to him. It was from Bavaria, from the Abbess of the hill-convent of Sancta Clara. This is what it said:

Sir:

This letter is written to you at the request of our very dear and cherished Sister Miranda, the late Princess of Wallenburg. I think you were a friend of hers. She

spoke often of you to me, but never to others. She said you
had been of help to her when she carried the crown of her
troubled reign. It may be therefore that you will care to
know of her life here and of her last days.

She was thin and frail when she came to us, worn by
her hard task, too heavy for her strength. But she was
very content to be with us,—happy in her heart and giving
happiness to others. She was extremely faithful in all the
small duties assigned to her. She seemed glad to be only
a Sister, not a Queen any more. But she wasted away and
faded month by month till she was almost like a sweet
shadow of herself.

Her religion was very simple and real to her. She was
constantly comforted by its practice and its hopes. You
will pardon me, dear Sir, for saying that I trust you share
these hopes. They are the only path to a happy immor-
tality. She prayed for you every day. This I know because she told me.

Her final days on earth were full of peace. She received
the last Sacrament with a sigh of deep content. At the
end her mind wandered a little through weakness. She
seemed to be trying to lift something from her head. She
said, "Please take it away, mother, it hurts me." I assured her that there was nothing there, and she grew
quieter. She asked, "Are there crowns in Heaven, and
must I wear one?" I told her they were crowns that had
no weight, more like wings than burdens. She said, "I'm
glad of that,—very, very glad. If our Lord commands me
I will take it." Then she murmured a few words of the
Nunc Dimittis, and fell asleep, and passed away.

Before her strength wholly failed she asked for a pencil
and with great effort wrote a few words for you. I am in
doubt about sending them. But after prayer it seems

right. She was my dearest niece, a good girl,—the best I ever knew. I love her forever in Christ. And so, I hope, do you.

Faithfully,

ADELAIDE, ABBESS OF SANCTA CLARA.

A half-sheet of thin paper fluttered to the floor. The man picked it up and read in tremulous letters: *"You have helped me—dearest friend—very good to me—do not forget—let us meet again—please God. Your M. A."*

Dabney took from the drawer of his desk an old-fashioned gold locket with his mother's miniature. He laid the folded paper in the back of the case and put it in the pocket over his heart. He stood a moment looking far into the rosy embers of the fire. Then he said to himself,—or was it to her? "I will, please God, I will."